Black Angel

A Novella By

Tay Shereé

Black Angel Copyright © 2013 Tay Shereé

All rights reserved. No part of this book may be reproduced in any form or by any means without prior consent of the Publisher, except brief quotes used in reviews.

ISBN 10: 1482585235
ISBN 13: 978-1482585230
Editor: Rubina Sardon

First Printing April 2013
Printed in the United States of America

10 9 8 7 6 5 4 3 2 1

This novella is a work of fiction. Any references to real people, events, establishments or locals are intended only to give the fiction a sense of reality and authenticity. Other names, characters, and incidents occurring in the work are either the product of the author's imagination or are used fictitiously, as those fictionalized events and incidents that involve real persons. Any character that happens to share the name of a person who is an acquaintance of the author, past or present, is purely coincidental and is in no way intended to be an actual account involving that person.

Dedication

I would like to dedicate my first book to my Stink, Rashad Sincere O'Neal. You have changed my life for the better and made me into the woman I am today. Everything that I do is for us baby. I want you to know that if nobody has your back your mommy does!

Acknowledgements

First I would like to thank God, my creator. Without him none of this would be possible. This has not been an easy journey but I kept the faith and it all worked out.

Next I would like to thank my mother Rubina Sardon for being there for me and most importantly for being a wonderful editor even though we had our differences through the process I still love her dearly. Author Shenetta Marie, my God mother, I would like to thank you for coaching me and believing in my skills. I know that I am not the easiest to deal with but look, we did it!

Keith Buchanan, my love. I have so much to say but what's understood doesn't need to be explained. You have listened to me whine, complain, and tell you over 100 times that I quit but you never let me. You believed in me even when I didn't. Your support is greatly appreciated.

Latasha Edwards, thank you for being the first to read over my book and giving me a great amount of feedback.

Now I would like to Shoutout my friends and family. Please forgive me if I forget anyone, it is not intentional.

My sisters come first. I love all eight of you: Shakeela, Ashauntae', Tania, Santajae, Lawren, Ronae, Ronnelle, Destiney.

My God sisters: B.Newton, Tanjenique, Kierra, Jalisa, Ashley C., Sharlisa and Qrica.

My God brothers, Nookie and Tae.

My God aunt Tamira Nannette, my hair dresser.

My God babies Virgil, my TT butt. Carter, Amyah, Demari Lashae, I love ya'll sooo much.

My good friends Bianca and Dizzy, I love you two to death. Danielle B., Shantell W., Essence S. My :Bri's" PMB Yurkiw and Briona P. I love you all!

My BGSU girls: Danica, Danayzha, Derricka, Eboni, my Jess's, and Shay Bay I miss you all soooo much! Continue to be successful. You all did it. Graduation May 4th, 2013! I am so proud of my girls.

My cousins Jennifer, Mellissa, and Regona.

Shardey We argue and fight like sisters but I would not trade them for the world. Pray for Kamyah!

Silly ass Dreski and Marcus Pearl. Where do I start with you two? My friends since 07 and we haven't fell out yet. You two have always checked on me over the years and I can always call on you when needed. Stay real!

Michael Gordon, my best friend. I am so happy that you went to the Navy to carry out your dreams. I love you and wish you the best of luck. I believe in you!

Most importantly I want to shout out Marlon Savion Hudson. We began this writing journey together and I am definitely going to carry it out for you. Free them Hudson boys!!!

From me to you!

Anyone can be an artist. Everyone has some artistic style in them you just have to know where to find it within yourself. You have chefs, painters, rappers, singers, etc. The most important of all artists to me is an author. Authors give you the written details that heighten everything. How can you imagine things with no description? I respect everyone's hustle; I support everyone, especially my Cleveland artist. My passion happens to be writing. People express their thoughts through music, sports, and many more ways but I get my thoughts out through my pen. It's so beautiful because you get lost between fantasy and reality. I am not perfect, I am flawed but I live vicariously through my characters. I am a good girl with bad thoughts. I AM BLACK ANGEL!

Prologue

Bang Bang! Shots reigned into the dark night of the city. Knight and Talia were on their way home from bullshitting around downtown at the Metrop and obviously some shit was about to pop off. Talia was very confused because she had never been so close to any real action like this before with Knight. She was used to street fights and arguments in the hood, on 131st but not a part of anything like this. This was the type of shit that people only read about in the paper or heard about on the news. Knight on the other hand was always ready for whatever. This was his normal everyday life. He kept his glock 40 on his waist and stayed ready for war. As they peeked around the building next to the parking lot they saw a group of men, six of them to be exact, wearing all black.

From Talia's view they all had eyes and appearances of killers. Right then she just wanted to take the clear shot to her truck and grab her gun but she knew that he wouldn't allow that and she was pissed. She was about to be caught slipping without it. Knight pushed her back with his muscular arm to keep her out of harm's way and the motion of his body turned her on. She wasn't used to this type of aggression from a man that she was attracted to but she knew that she liked it. She felt protected by Knight so she trusted him. She stayed tucked behind him as he looked around the side of the building.

What he saw was Reds crew making a drop off to Los's crew. Reds crew was from around the way so it made sense why the deal was being made at that very spot. Within two seconds Reds head soldier pulled out his

Tay Sheree

sawed off shot gun and shot Los right in his chest. Knight already knew it was gone be some trouble on St. Clair now since one of the biggest dope dealers in the city was taken out. He immediately pulled Talia close to him and made himself a human shield for her which he couldn't even believe he was doing. Right now she needed her own piece. *What happened to protect yourself at all times* she thought to herself.

The shots continued from both sides for about ten minutes and then it was complete silence. Knight slowly rose from on top of Talia's petite body and looked around the garage again. Shit got real. It was bodies everywhere and not one soul was living to tell, at least he thought. Knight shook his head in disbelief but then quickly came to reality and scoped out the scene. He didn't want Talia to see any of this because he thought that she would lose it but she didn't and he was surprised. When she saw all of the blood pools that is when she lost it. He instantly covered her mouth to block out the squeals she was releasing and to keep away unwanted attention. As many times as she had been around killings, blood still bothered her. She was shocked and scarred after what her ears and eyes just witnessed. All she could do was look around and make sure no one was coming toward her once Knight let her go.

The parking garage was so quiet and empty which was unusual because there is usually an attendant there but no one came. While she was still sitting there in shock Knight pulled out his handy gloves. With all of the shit he gets into he always keeps a pair of gloves close. He

Black Angel

preferred gloves from any hospital, not any dollar store bullshit because they made him feel like they were more legit. He never liked real cheap shit anyway. Rule #1 Leave no fingerprints. He immediately tied up his hood, put on his gloves, then grabbed every bag possible then went back to grab Talia. He already had it in his head that he would have to teach her some things about the streets after this shit died down but he never expected to get her involved in his lifestyle so soon. He didn't want to at all but eventually she would have to be put on to game if she would be fucking with him. Talia finally snapped back into reality and helped Knight carry the bags as they left the scene as quickly as possible without being noticed. Rule #2 was to never look suspicious. Knight spotted a familiar face right after he loaded Talia's 2011 Lexus LX570 but he ignored them and refused to make eye contact. He didn't tell her about it either because she might panic or get them noticed. Talia was moving like she had done this shit before and Knight couldn't help but wonder why it was so easy to her. Baby girl had heart.

Sirens were just now approaching the lot. Talia shook a little more. Knight glanced over and knew that he had to take care of her. As they pulled away from the parking garage six police cars and two ambulances came on the scene. As Talia thought her life was over Knight knew that their life had just began and that they had came up on The Perfect Lick...

ଔଔଔଔଔଔ

Jay Sheree

I hate working on Friday's man. The phone never stops fucking ringing. Just ring ring ring and no real action. Not anything that I care about anyways. Where's the fucking action? I can't sit at this desk any longer. Some asshole has to be fucking up somewhere, anywhere! Williams thought to himself as he sat at his desk.

The 3rd district received a tip call. There was some sort of drug deal that was going down and Williams wanted parts. Williams had been working for the city of Cleveland for 12 years now and for the past three he has been on desk duty which would end today. He had a history of anger issues and the captain had finally benched him for beating someone during an arrest. Williams impatiently waited at the captain's door to confirm that he would be taking on that mission and conveniently his partner Davis walked past so he got his attention.

Davis was considered a rookie to everyone else and the district. He has only been there for a year and a half. Even though Williams dreaded training the "new guy", he knew that doing so would be his best bet at getting away from that desk. Williams convinced the captain that he should be able to be on duty with Davis and the captain allowed them. That was where the captain made his first mistake because Williams was not ready to be back on the streets. Before heading to the scene Davis replayed the recording from the dispatcher so that they knew exactly what they were getting in to.

Dispatcher: *Is there a threat to your life or your property?*

Black Angel

Old lady: I wouldn't say all that but these niggas is out here doing drug deals across from my god damned house in this parking garage. I warned them more than once to stop that shit.
Dispatcher: Are you or someone else the victim of a crime?
Old lady: No. But I sure as hell don't want to be a witness either.
Dispatcher: Do you or someone else have a medical emergency?
Old lady: Well if one of these crack heads overdose ya'll gone be looking mighty crazy and I don't want anything to do with it.
Dispatcher: Do you need the fire dept?
Old lady: Unless you plan on hosing one of these young motherfuckas into your custody then no! Bring the police and the goddamn S.W.A.T. while you are at.
Dispatcher: Ma'am where are you and these men located?
Old lady: Look while you're asking all of these questions you wasting time. You're the one with the fancy ass caller i.d. so I'm sure you already know where I am. Just get here and get here quick something is about to happen

ଔଔଔଔଔଔ

  Williams and Davis arrived on the scene and started to question the old lady who made the 911 call to their precinct.
  "Take over Rookie." Williams told Davis while he went to make a phone call.
  He realized where they were so he had to make sure that he checked on some shit. Davis took over interviewing the witness while Williams stepped to the side and made a

Tay Sheree

suspicious call. The witness was highly upset because she made herself clear to the dispatcher that the police needed to get there asap but they took too long. She didn't want those pigs at her home anyways. Williams and Davis found out that shots had already been fired so they cut the lady off and fled straight to the parking garage. When they got there it was too late. All of the young niggas were either dead or they scattered. Williams and Davis were not to touch anything until they had some back up so Williams called for them immediately. In the meantime they just looked around without touching anything. At least Davis wasn't touching anything. Williams was searching for Los's phone.

Davis: *This is Davis and I need back up to 5485 East 9th Street.*
Dispatcher: *Roger that. They will be on their way to you as soon as possible sir.*

Davis spotted a tall man with his hood up hopping into a truck nearby. He couldn't make out what exactly the man was doing but he felt that he was suspicious.

"Aye Williams, check this out right here. It looks like he's trying to get away with something. Let's go get his ass!"

"Man he ain't got nothing to do with this shit over here. He doesn't even look concerned that we're over here. Most niggas would've started running by now. You know how they are."

"I mean, but i'm just saying sir, I think that we should at least question him."

Black Angel
"What the hell did I just say? Either shut yo ass up or go do it yourself."

"Sir, you know I can't approach a suspect alone."

"Well I guess your only other option is to shut up then." He said through a chuckle.

Soon after that their backup arrived and Davis ran over to follow and learn as much as possible.

"What do we have here Officer Williams?"

"Umm sir we have 5 DOA's and no suspects."

"So you mean to tell me not one asshole stuck around to steal anything?" Officer Davis attempted to alert the captain that there was a possible suspect but Williams quickly cut him off, "No, sir. There was no one on or around the scene when we arrived." He cut his eyes at Davis as if he was threatening him.

"Somebody had to take something because there is no way that this scene is spotless. Something is missing. What the hell was the motive? Why do I have 5 dead people in my precinct?" The captain yelled as he kept circling the crime scene to see if he would notice anything else unusual.

Davis was really frustrated and confused now because he wasn't sure if he should let the captain know what he had seen. Telling him now could get the both of them in trouble. From now on he knew that he would have to speak up when it came to working with Davis because he doesn't play nice. While the squad took pictures and notes Davis tried to come up with scenarios over and over in his head. *That man that I saw had to have something to do with this. I know he did. I just have to figure out what.*

Tay Sheree

"Rookie!" The captain yelled from across the lot. What do you see wrong with this crime scene?"

"Well sir, there is really no evidence so we need to find out what these men were all here for. Was there a party, was it a drug deal gone wrong, or what."

"Good job Rookie. You're one smart kid. Keep up the good work." The way that Williams was staring at Davis you would have thought that they were long lost enemies instead of partners.

He didn't like the fact that Davis was a smart ass. He felt like he was showing out and that he should be asked the questions because he was the vet. Fuck this young nigga. Williams had fucked up a case before so the captain was iffy about trusting him again. *Why does this motherfucka get all of the attention? He don't know shit. But that's cool cuz these bitches got to pay me regardless.* He stood there with a smirk on his face and let his partner get all of the attention that he thought he deserved.

All of the detectives finished cleaning and packing up the scene. Everybody was carried out in body bags. This would be some crazy shit to see on Fox 8 news in the morning. 5 members from two separate gangs were killed by each other with no known suspects. Ain't that some shit to hear. At the end, the captain called a meeting to discuss the status of the case.

"Team, we are now looking for any leads on missing money, drugs, and guns. If you find anyone or anything you immediately report to me. It now seems that someone or more than one person has got away with some very

Black Angel

important merchandise." Everyone agreed except Williams.

He had some plans of his own if he came up with any leads. He wanted and needed his hands on some money and he did not plan on getting it by legal means. *Fuck the captain and anybody else who ain't with me. I need this paper and I'm gone get it by any means, the fuck they thought. Let me catch the bitch ass niggas who got away with the shit and it's curtains. It's cool. The streets talk baby so believe that. I'll find out and I will shut shit down!* Williams thought to himself as the squad left the scene.

Chapter One

These bitches know I don't like these ghetto ass bars. I can't believe they brought me to The Gotcha. Talia thought as she strut her long slim legs to the door. She was 5'3 and a solid 136lbs. Her body was very toned and athletic like. She had deep brown eyes so deep that you could see her hidden pain in them. Her skin was milk chocolate and so smooth. What most attracted people to her were her lips. They were succulent lips that have a natural outline as if she wore lip liner.

As usual her skin was natural with no makeup. Earlier that day she went to the nail shop to get her usual athletic length French tip on top of her natural nails. Then she went to her aunt Nette's house to get her eyebrows arched and her hair done in a 24inch genie ponytail with a swooped bang. Nette always hooked her up and got her hair together according to Talia's outfits that she would wear. Talia's diamond studded nose ring accentuated her hair and her outfit.

That night she would be sporting an all black, side mesh Michael Kors dress with some spiked Christian Louboutin heels that accented her long mocha legs. On her wrist was a Michael Kors watch that Jay had bought her for Christmas two years ago and she also wore the matching earrings. You couldn't tell her fly ass nothing even though to her that outfit was simple and comfortable.

Kamari wore a real short all black Christian Dior dress that flawlessly snugged her nice ass and wide hips. People always said that she had baby making hips but Kamari had no intentions on letting any children mess with hers. Her heelless wedges accented her curvy calves and made her look like a stallion. Talia got her hair together for the night and she was rocking some 14" loose body waves that hung over her shoulders.

Nikki liked to be simple but even when she didn't want attention she still drew it. She wore black also but she had on a gray,high waist, Ralph Lauren pencil skirt that hugged her ass so properly. She wore an all black Ralph Lauren blazer with just a bra underneath it. Her blazer had her 36 D's sitting pretty. Nikki didn't have a normal ass. Niggas stayed fantasizing about her so alot of times she tried to stay covered up but it was no hiding her shape. It didn't make it any better that she had long natural bone straight hair that hung to her ass. She was so obsessed with it that she would not even let Talia put any color in it. All of her bitches were gorgeous!

Talia loved her childhood friends and would kill ANY and she meant anybody for them. Everybody hated them but nobody wanted to do anything about it. Until then they would continue to do them with their pretty asses.

When they got in the bar the first thing they did was take pictures. The thing that they all dreaded was taking a picture too late when their hair was all sweated out. So, what better time to take them than soon as they hit the door? The picture man was in awe when the three beautiful women stepped in front of him and automatically posed. Talia handed him sixty dollars.

"Three poses."

Black Angel

"They're ten a piece ma'am." The picture man tried to tell her.

"Well keep the change then." She laughed at him as they continued to get into their places.

Their cockiness was giving this soft ass camera man a hard on and his weak ass loved the show. First Talia stood in the middle and she stood to the side so that you got the whole view of her legs. Next Nicole was in the middle and she made sure that you got a clear view of her ass.

"Un uh! Let me see that picture before you keep that. I need to make sure I don't look fat." The camera man was thirsty to respond.

"You don't look fat baby, you look perfectly fine." He said trying to kiss her ass in hopes of getting her name and number knowing damn well that he would never have a chance with any of them.

"First of all, I am not your baby and second of all I know I'm not fat boo boo, I was just saying." Nikki said with her smart ass mouth while rolling her neck.

She was like that all of the time but the thing about it was none of these hoes had the balls to shut her up. The three of them switched sides again while cracking up after Nikki gave the picture man the okay to take the next and last picture. This time Kamari was in the middle and the poses switched up. Kamari was thick and cold. She reminded you of Emily B. Her girls already knew how this picture would be taken and Talia and Nikki just waited to see the picture man's face. He said ya'll ready and they all looked at each other.

Tay Sheree

"Yea, we hope you are."

That's when Kamari bent right over just enough so that you couldn't see her underwear, Nikki smacked Kamari's ass right as the camera snapped and Talia was leaned forward with her middle finger up and her tongue out showing her diamond studded tongue ring. The camera man's face was priceless as well as everyone else in the bar. All eyes were on them and they loved it right now. If they weren't in front of the camera, every eye that was laid on them would have been dealt with. They had to take a crazy picture any time that they went out to remember and cherish every moment that they had together. You never know when someone can leave you.

They finally made it to the dance floor. They usually skipped the bar because they believed in drinking before they made it to their destination so that they could feel themselves early. They always wound up at the bar for at least one drink before they left though to have either an incredible hulk or a blue motherfucka. But if Talia was buting she always bought doubles of Ciroc. Two shots for each of them. She never hung out with different crews; it was her bitches or no one.

As they danced on the floor Talia felt some eyes on her. If she didn't learn anything from her ex he definitely taught her to always watch her back, no matter if you are in the car, on foot, or on any scene. You never know who is watching you. Her suspicions were right. Some fine ass man had his eyes on her and she kind of liked the attention. She moved her body elegantly with the music and she was definitely feeling herself. Dance music and R&B always put

Black Angel

her in a good mood. Talia loved to dance since she was a little girl. There was one point in time where you couldn't stop her ass from dancing. His eyes never left her even though there were so many other people in there. When the song went off she thought to herself; *why me out of all of these other bitches in here. I know i'm attractive but damn, he hasn't taken his eyes off of me yet.*

"Aye ya'll look. Theses niggas over here staring at us."

"Shiiit. Let's put on a show for their asses then." Kamari was always down to act a fool with her girls. "Wait a minute. That's Knight and his boys. They ain't bout shit. I hear Knight a killer. The last time that I checked he had a girl."

"Oh really? I can't tell cuz he sure staring me down." Talia was agitated that he was even looking her way now. She hated cheaters.

The crew of niggas continued to watch them dance to Jeezy. As time went past they separated and then it was just one of them by himself that seemed to still have his eye on Talia. She really didn't know how to feel about that now knowing that he supposedly has a girlfriend but she just kept on dancing until she decided that she needed another drink.

"Come on ya'll, I need another drink!" She yelled over the music to her friends and they happily followed.

"What we sipping on now?" Nikki asked.

"I'm thinking CocoLoso tonight." Talia said and her girls agreed.

Tay Shereé

CocoLoso was her favorite drink now. It was simply Coconut Ciroc and Pineapple juice. Her favorite rapper, Fabolous introduced her to it and she's been addicted since. Hell, she even drinks it during the week because it's so smooth.

As Talia ordered the drinks she felt someone, someone taller and much bigger than her standing over her. She took her time turning around as she reached for her glock 19 just to find out that she had left it in her truck. When she turned around she saw that it was the man who had been staring at her since they had been there. *Finally he's approaching me. I was starting to wonder if he was just a creeper or something. I'm glad he's not though cuz he's too fine for that shit. I didn't wanna have to take his ass out in front of all of these people.* Then the voice that she had been waiting to hear, finally spoke.

"Hello beautiful." She melted and then it all began. They conversed then headed to their seats.

I can't believe it took him so long to say something to me. He must have been waiting to see if I was here waiting on somebody. Ha, proved him wrong. I'm single as a dollar baby. Talia Marie don't have time to be answering to no nigga. I'm ALL about this paper baby. You know what matter of fact I'm about to give this nigga a run for his money. He's been watching me since I got here. He thinks he's slick. She thought to herself as they walked across the bar.

Chapter Two

It was a Saturday night and Lalo (Knights bestfriend), was throwing a party at the Gotcha. Everybody knew Lalo so it was definitely about to go down. Niggas was getting dressed, throwing on their flyest fits, and taking shots at the same damn time! Knight didn't smoke much because he said it made him do crazy shit and everyone knew that Knight was naturally crazy so no one even encouraged it.

Ring Ring! The cell phone rang. Knight looked at the screen and it was Ronnelle, his ex girlfriend. He ignored it. Ronnelle moved to L.A. and had a baby on him so he couldn't bring himself to be in love with her again. Yea, he still had love for her but things could never be the same. He hadn't told her that yet but he had planned on it. They were together since they were younger but things just weren't working out for them so he felt the best way to deal with it was to ignore her but he knew that he would never hear the end of it. She moved to Cali with her mother when they graduated from Glenville high school since Knight had no intentions on moving her in to his home. He was always ahead of everyone his age and by the time that he was 17 he was already renting to own a house. She was his main bitch. He even made trips out there from time to time to check on her despite their differences.

Ronnelle and Knight could never move forward right now because he still wanted that single life and forced himself to keep Ronnelle off of his mind. But at the same time he still needed her but she wasn't having it. He cheated and she did too so many times that they should

Tay Sheree

have left each other alone years ago but their love was so strong that they just couldn't shake one another for good. He always came back around at the perfect time which really urked her nerves.

His phone vibrated and a message came across his screen. It read, *You must be going out with them weak ass friends tonight. Don't think I don't know that it's Lalo's birthday. Let me catch you out in any other bitch face. It's over with for you and her, believe that!* And Ronnelle meant every word that she said and Knight knew it.

He read the text message, still mindful of what she said, and then continued to get dressed. He knew not to cross her but he really did need to stay away from her.

He decided that he would break it off with her in the morning when he was sober again so that she wouldn't think that he was still drunk or on no bullshit. This here had to end, fuck all of the bullshit. He could no longer deal with the insecurities, the lying that he was doing, and all of the pain that he was causing her. *Breaking it off would be the best thing for us right now right? I love her too much to keep hurting her. She should understand. I hope she understands. I don't know hoiw I'm going to break this off. I love Ronnelle too much to do her bad cuz we've been through so much together. These secret trips to see her have to end. I'm even hiding the shit from my best friend. I really need to figure this out quick.*

Lalo sat his drink down so he could tend to his friend. They were like blood brothers. He could sense the sad and irritated vibe that was coming from Knight. Lalo and Knight had been friends since before they were even born. Knight's mother and Lalo's father were good friends

Black Angel

from high school. Lalo is only 6 months older than Knight. Since their parents lived next door from each other they were bound from the start. They were inseparable. If you had beef with one you best to believe you had war with the other. But they had their share of fights too. It was always a challenge of who was stronger or faster. It was no doubt that Lalo was faster but strength, Knight had that on lock. Niggas knew they didn't want problems with Lalo on the fighting side and they damn sure wasn't coming Knights way. He would knock a nigga out without him knowing it was any beef. He was young, reckless, and simply just didn't give a fuck.

"My nigga what's good? Ronnelle got yo head fucked up again. You tryna stay in and text her all night?" Lalo said in his most sarcastic voice ever.

"Fuck you nigga. You just mad cuz you ain't got a bitch to even worry about yo ugly ass." Knight said coming back at Lalo for that bold insult.

"You right. I don't have a bitch cuz I got all the bitches my nigga and I could have your Ms. "Hollywood" too if I wanted her high class ass."

"Be my guest. I'm tryna get her up off of my hands anyway."

"You know you love that girl man, chill out."

"Yea, but our love ain't make that baby she out there taking care of and it sure ain't making me no money either so she gotta go."

"Word?"

Tay Sheree

"Word like a mufucka." Knight said with slight hurt in his voice but he had to do what needed to be done and that was to leave Ronnelle.

The crew was ready to go but most of all Knight was. *Man, i'm drunk and feeling myself, I need some pussy! I can't go to Ronnelle house and my old freak mad at me. Man what the fuck am I talking about? I wasn't gone travel to Cali for none either* (he laughed to himself). *I'm not tryna fuck none of these hoes from the club either. Aye. Pussy is pussy I get it when I need it.*

"Turn up niggas!" Lalo screamed out loud in the lot.

"I'm ready to shut shit down and fuck with these niggas bitches, man. Ya'll betta be ready cuz I'm out here." Knight started up his all black 2004 Denali as he thought *I hope these fools ain't on no bullshit tonight,* and then they were headed out to see what the land had to offer.

౹౹౹౹౹౹

I'm way too gone what the fuck am I doing. Wake up in the morning, who the fuck am I screwing? My partner on brown and you know I'm on white. You know it's going down, I can do this all night…..

Jeezy played loud through the speakers of the club and Knight was for sure feeling his self. He fucks with Young Jeezy the long way and that song put him on ten. He was now in his zone and you couldn't tell him nothing. The crew was walking around straight thugging, cooling, and fucking with the bitches. Knight needed to get his mind off of Ronnelle so he was on the prowl. As he scoped

Black Angel

the club from his bar stool, he laid his eyes on one beautiful girl. She was so chocolate and her skin was glistening. Knight couldn't take his eyes off of her. *Who the fuck is that? I've never seen her around here before. Shit, it doesn't even matter cuz after tonight she gone be mine. I can't let her get away. Damn she is gorgeous!* Talia turned her head and she caught him staring at her. She wasn't shy at all so she put on a show for him. She danced so sexy and swagged it out for the whole song and he never took his eyes off of her. Watching her move her body perfectly to every beat was making him rock hard and he couldn't take it anymore. Lalo walked up on him, pushed him in the shoulder and got him out of his trance.

"Aye nigga! You're staring mighty hard at that bitch over there. Who is that with her black ass?" He was laughing his ass off.

"She ain't no bitch, nigga! And I don't know her. I'm gone find out who she is though and whoever her nigga is he chalked off rip."

"How you know she even got a nigga?"

"I don't. But as bad as she is I wouldn't believe her if she didn't."

"Alright man. Don't fall in love in this club, ol' Usher head ass nigga."

"Nigga fuck you wit yo weak ass." He chuckled because he couldn't help but laugh at Lalo's stupid ass jokes.

He couldn't stand there anymore joking with Lalo wasting time because his possible Queen would get away and he wasn't having that. Knight was never a scary nigga.

21

Tay Shereé

He approaches basic and bad bitches on the daily but for some reason this girl was different and that was what made him want this stranger even more. He stared from her legs all the way up to her beautiful face several more times before their eyes connected. He saw her yell to her friends and they started to head to the bar. Then was the perfect time for him to approach her.

"Hello beautiful."

"Hello, and your name is?"

"Damn Ma, why the attitude but my name is Knight. How come i've never seen you around here?"

"My name is Talia Marie and I don't know why you haven't seen me around here. I don't come here often but I don't recognize you either." She played dumb. She knew exactly who he was because she had heard how much of a boss that he was in the streets.

"Well hopefully I get to see you more often then Ms. Talia, I would love to spend more time with you."

"Why are you being so nice to me? What is it that you want? It's so many other females in here and you chose me to talk to, yea, that's somewhat fishy."

"Aw man come on don't do me like that. You don't have confidence or something you're beautiful baby I just want to talk to you."

"Yes, I have confidence but I was just curious."

"That's cool too. Let's sit over here and talk, too many people are staring at us."

Talia's friends Kamari and Nikki stared at Knight as they were being nosey and listened to him try to seduce their best friend.

Black Angel

"Gone head girl. Call us when you leave so we can make sure your Knight got you home." Kamari said as her and Nikki laughed and Talia knew how sarcastic and petty they were so she couldn't help but laugh with her childhood friends.

Knight walked behind Talia as they headed to the booth admiring her long legs as they moved. The whole bar watched them. Not only because they knew of Knight's history with Ronnelle but because together they looked gorgeous. Ronnelle knocked out over a dozen bitches out in that very bar for just looking Knight's way. His smooth dark skin and her smooth glossy dark skin kept everybody's eyes rolling and going. They were the "couple" that everybody wanted to be right now. Knight was borderline conceited so he loved the way the eyes were on them and Talia was the opposite she was ready to pop each and every bitch or nigga that laid eyes on her. She wasn't for all of that attention bullshit because to her if you were staring you either just wanted to fuck her or you were jealous, period.

They finally reached the booth and Knight held out his hand to help her in to her seat first. She kept a straight face but inside she was melting. She couldn't believe that this hard looking dude was actually so nice like this and he didn't even know her. The way that he acted you would have thought that they were a couple for years. *Damn, this boy got me gone and I ain't even hit that yet. This thirst is real on my end. I ain't no sucka though so let me fuck his head up cuz whatever he looking for it ain't happening!* Talia thought as she stared up and down Knights sexy athletic body while he

Tay Sheree

ordered their drinks from the server named Kelly that came over to see if they were good on drinks.

Knight stood 5'8, not as tall as the dudes that she usually talked to but he was perfect. As long as he could stand over her head she was cool with it. His hair was cut real low but he had enough hair to get brush waves and man were they spinning. His face was clean, none of that rough neck facial hair. You could tell that he took pride in his appearance. He had broad shoulders like those ones you see on the men that were locked up and worked out all day.

His arms were so sexy and just the right size. She wanted to make love to his biceps! You could even tell how cut he was through his True Religion t-shirt. She was so drawn to his kind eyes. They were so fierce and intense enough to see right through anyone. Her eyes kept going from his body to his hands. His hands were so strong but gentle. One of Talia's turn offs was a man with hands as soft as hers. He sat next to her so confident as if he knew Talia was watching him. He just turned to her and smiled.

This motherfucka don't even know what I drink so how is he ordering anything for me. Well i'm picky so I hope he makes a good choice. She thought to herself while still holding that same straight face.

"Hey. Who told you that I like blue dot Ciroc?" She said because she had overheard even though that was one of her favorite drinks.

"No one it was a wild guess. But you don't look like a dark liquor type of girl and I don't wanna be the reason you somewhere acting crazy even though I don't mind taking care of you." His full mouth of beautiful white teeth was showing. Talia couldn't help but smile back because she was so comfortable sitting in a bar with him as if they did this before.

As they were talking Kelly came back over and placed their orders on coasters. "There you go. Let me know if you need anything else." She took their money and walked away.

"Well, little do you know I am also a Henn type of girl. Straight. No chaser!" She winked then took her shot.

His dick jumped at her cockiness. This girl was something special. He had to figure out what the catch was. Most beautiful girls are some sort of crazy.

"Okay, last round on me." She pulled a wad of fifties and twenties out of her purse and began to put a fifty dollar bill on the counter.

Knight had seen females with money before but this much had him thinking. Before she could even motion for the waitress again he shot cold eyes at her that made her scared to pay for anything else in her life.

"Please don't ever do that again. If a nigga invites you anywhere and lets you foot the bill he's a bitch and tell him Knight said that shit." He said in the most serious voice that he had.

"Okay." Was all she could say because she obviously could not but still would not argue with him.

Both of them had aggressive, cocky attitudes and that's just a few of the things that attracted them to each other. Talia had never been talked to like that before and the shit turned her on major.

Jay Shereé

Every other nigga that she had talked to let her be the aggressor and she didn't like that shit at all. She needed a real man who was aggressive, book and street smart, just like how every man wants his woman. Knight paid for their last drinks with no questions asked and that was that. They sat in their booth, drank, and talked for about an hour more not realizing that the bar was about to close anyway. Even though they were sitting right there when the bartender called out the last call on drinks, they did not hear anything but each other. Neither one of them had experienced this kind of connection in years. Talia's phone vibrated and interrupted their conversation.

"Excuse me." She said as she opened her message hoping that it wasn't Jay's ass calling her after she told him to lose her number. Jay was her ex boyfriend that she was trying to shake. *Don't forget you have an interview tomorrow, do not be late Marie.* The message from her mother read. Her mother always called her by her middle name when it was important.

"Damn it's getting late, I didn't even know." Talia squealed as she jumped up. Knight was startled by how fast she got up that he popped up too.

"What's wrong? You got a man to get home to or something?" He had slight disgust in his voice.

"No baby, it's nothing like that. I have an interview in the morning." She said as she moved swiftly as if she was missing something.

Baby? I like the sound of that even if she didn't mean it. He was so shocked by what she said that he didn't even realize that she was talking to him again.

Black Angel

"Um hello...Are you there? She snapped her finger as if he was in a trance. Are you ready to go?"

"Aww shit, yea. Come on chocolate we out of here." Before they walked out of the door she texted her friends to let them know that she was safe and on her way home. *Girls I'm safe. He is too cool. I'm headed home now. Call you guys in the a.m. All smiles!* Talia sent out a group message knowing but then again not knowing how safe she would really be that night. She had no idea that her life would change the day that she met Knight.

Chapter Three

The Perfect Lick

After all of their drinks and conversation Talia had to get ready for bed so that she could make it to her big interview tomorrow and Knight was trying to get back to some money. Talia had been looking for jobs since she wanted to get out of the streets. She didn't want just any job; she had to be making big money. Somewhere with one of those fancy desk with her name on it was where she needed to be. She had too much talent to go to waste. On the other hand, Knight had no intentions on getting out any time soon. He was all about his money and she was all about being successful. Fast money excited him though the shit still didn't come easy. She wasn't in the streets purposely. She did it because she had to in order to survive. She had always dreamed of being a nurse and now she had the opportunity to work for Cleveland Clinic. Knight was all for Talia wanting to be successful too so he was in a rush to make sure she that got home in a timely manner.

They were in the process of walking to where they had both parked their trucks when they heard two gunshots nearby. Knight was used to shit like this on St.Clair so he immediately pushed Talia back and peeked around the corner. Inside of a parking garage some fucked up shit was about to go down that he really did not want to be a part of so he kept his distance but still tuned in and Talia was right there by his side just as alert. Even if he

Tay Sheree

wasn't directly a part of the deal he would be indirectly because Knight knew these niggas from the hood and he would take them out if he had to, to get a hold of whatever money or drugs they had. Knight was a greedy nigga who wanted nothing but to stay on top of the game. He knew them but really could give a fuck about them because they weren't in his circle.

ଔଔଔଔଔଔ

"Where the fuck is my money Los?" Red said adamantly.

"I got it man, I got it. It's in the case that one of my soldiers is holding." He said with a smirk because he thought that he was about to get over on Red.

Los had four soldiers with him. One had a case full of guns, the next had counterfeit money, one had the real money that Red was looking for, and his last soldier was just big as fuck and there for security purposes. Red didn't like the fact that Los was trying to play games with him so he had to take him out. Nobody played with Reds money and then Los had the audacity to call Red like he was about his shit. *I knew I shouldn't have gave this bitch ass nigga the time of day just to waste my fuckin' time. He must've thought he was gone get away with my money and my supply. Kill yourself nigga. Better yet let me do it!* Red said to himself before he signaled his head soldier Cordero to take Los out.

"Alright Los, bring me the money. Soldier, give this nigga what he came here for." Red said as Los walked up

Black Angel

with his empty suitcase as if he was really making an exchange. He was really giving one of his soldiers the que to take Red out then keep their eye on the rest of his crew. Then pow pow, two shots were fired and everybody looked around to see what niggas got popped not knowing what the fuck had happened. Los hit the ground first because he got shot right in between his eyes then Red coughed up some blood and his soldiers were furious but still confused. Why was Red still standing on his two feet if he got hit? He got hit right in his chest with the shot gun, not through enough to kill him instantly but it was good enough to take him out. Before Red fell to his demise he managed to get out, "kill these bitch ass niggas and get my shit somewhere safe!" Then he dropped and fell over while holding his nuts just like the OG that he was. All he had was his balls and his word and his word was bond.

He wanted Los dead and there he was laying lifeless right across from him. If he couldn't make money in his streets then no one else could except HIS young niggas if he had anything to do with it. Everyone from Los crew was confused as to what Red was speaking on before he died and that started the riot. Even though they didn't know exactly what he was talking about they knew that it had to be important if he made that his last words. Both sets emptied bullets off into each other and into the air until no one was standing. The only one who got away was Cordero. He couldn't get a hold of Reds belongings at the time with all of the shooting so he figured once everyone

Tay Sheree was dead or gone that he would come back to collect everything, that was before the police arrived of course. *Shit, I gotta get baby girl outta here before shit gets worse. I feel bad that she has to even see this shit. I gotta do something, quick!* Knight thought as he peeped the scene and started to grab the suitcases. Cordero was ordered by Red to go back and get the shit that Knight was now collecting for keeps. He wasn't going ot give any nigga the chance to come out on top over him. Red was the plug so he knew that he came up on some shit. Talia was still anxious because she really didn't know Knight so she kept her eyes on him to see what his next move would be. She didn't want to seem soft to Knight but this shit was out of control. *Why the fuck did I even agree to come with this nigga. I could have died or had to take this nigga out. What if my phone would have rang? I could be lying next to one of these dead people. I want to go home i'm pissed!* So many thoughts raced through her head as she watched Knight get all of the suitcases.

    She watched him as he handled everything with care. He put on gloves, *wait this motherfucka carries gloves.* She thought as she kept her eyes on him. He put his hood up, and he moved so swiftly. In no time he was back in front of her getting ready to motion her to take him to her vehicle but before he could say anything she was already headed to it. She was used to craziness that came with hood niggas so she already knew what was up. She popped the locks for him to hop in. He loaded the cases in her backseat on the floor and hopped in.

Black Angel

"You cool to drive?" He asked her before she pulled off.

She shot an irritated look at him and simply said "Where are we going?" She pulled out of the lot like nothing had just happened.

Knight was really feeling her. He was confused as to why she was so calm like she had done shit like this before but he was still feeling his liquor so he would forget after a while. She kept her cool and didn't flip on this nigga for putting her life in danger instead she had other plans. She would have parts of whatever he did. He didn't plan on making her go through any bullshit like that again but he knew that just in case he could count on her. Even though he had just met her he could tell that she was a real rider and that he didn't have to worry about having to take her out for snitching because Lord knows he did not want to but Knight was all about business and if you fucked him over you had to face the consequences. Just as he was thinking about taking her out if she seemed faulty she was thinking the same thing as they drove to his house. Family, friend, wife, or whatever. Yea, straight like that Knight and Talia were killers but only when they had to be. Snitches or the weak don't make it long where they come from.

Talia had noticed an all black Grand Marquis with its lights flashing pull in as they were getting ready to pull out but she never mentioned it to Knight because the less she said to him the better. She was going to get rid of this truck as soon as possible since it was now hot. They didn't need any unwanted attention on them especially not knowing what's in the suitcases. He could possibly do Fed time for this. What's more fucked up about the situation is that she would be going down too for some shit that she had nothing to do with. The shit didn't belong to Knight to begin with. She was still confused as to why she hadn't left that nigga in the garage before anything even happened. She was all out of her element for this nigga that she just met.

They had to get away from that scene. The longer they stayed around there the hotter they were becoming. Knight was worried about getting them somewhere safe and stashing these suitcases while Talia was worried about figuring out what the hell he had in them. Her head was now pounding with agonizing pain. She couldn't tell if it was from the liquor, the gun shots, or the loud music but she was still confused about her whole night. Like "why her" was all she could think. She felt like she was in some sick ass romance movie and she just prayed that this was the end of it and that they could walk away and never have to talk about this again. But this was all the beginning. Before she knew it Knight had led her to one of his houses. She checked out the whole house as they were pulling up and all she could say was damn.

Knight had two houses. One of them was for personal which was deep in Shaker heights and one for business, which was for strictly business. She wanted to ask how he got the money to buy this nice ass house but she knew that wasn't her business and she already knew the answer. That nigga was clearly heavy in the streets so she knew he had no intentions on telling any of his business.

Black Angel

Something wasn't right though and he knew it. He felt a strange vibe coming from her but he already knew what was up. Game recognizes game and Talia definitely had something on her mind. Talia did not know him yet and she was panicking so he could only respect that. She didn't show it much he just knew that she didn't trust him yet. Knight just played it cool and kept his eye on her. The last thing he needed was for her to sneak attack on some crazy shit and stab him or shoot his ass. You can never put anything past anyone. She dared Knight to try her because she felt like he thought she was a sucka but she had other plans for his ass if he jumped stupid.

Chapter Four

Talia stood outside of her truck while Knight grabbed the suitcases out of her backseat. He motioned for her to follow him in the house.

"Let me get my purse first." She purposely left her purse on the seat so that she had an excuse to go back and grab her gun from under her seat without being so obvious.

She then stepped in the house behind Knight and it was gorgeous but she couldn't take her mind off of the fact that she just basically hit a lick with this man and they barely knew each other. The only thing that went through her mind was him killing her and running off somewhere with whatever he had found if it was worth something. She wanted to know what it was. She thought about what she would do for a while but she went with her first mind and went with what she knew.

"Drop the suitcases motherfucka!"

Click click! She pulled her little Glock 19 out on Knight, pointed it at his spine and demanded that he drop the shit. His back was still to her and he smiled as he did what she said. The shit turned him on that she was even bold enough to pull some shit like this. But he gave her what she wanted to make her feel better about the situation. He knew that she wouldn't shoot him. Why come in the house with him to begin with.

"You sure this is what you want?" He asked as he slowly turned to face her with the gun never leaving his body.

"Don't come any closer man. I am not scared to shoot you." He kept coming closer to her letting her gun rest right on his sternum and she took a step back.

"What do you want from me?"

"Ma, I don't want anything from you. What's the problem? Why you uppin' strap on me girl?" He asked as he laughed at her.

"This shit is not funny. What the fuck is in those suitcases and what do you plan on doing with me?" She blurted out wanting as many answers as possible.

"Idk. I'm just as confused as you. Let's find out." He told her as he turned back around but she never stopped pointing her gun at him.

He was getting pissed off because she had that gun pointed at him still and he always felt like if you were going to point a gun at him then you better shoot him. So he caught her off guard and grabbed her wrist and gun.

"Next time you pull this lil shit out on me you better use it." He snatched her gun away.

Talia felt like a straight bitch. If she was in her right state of mind she would have never let no shit like that go down. He pulled her hoe card and she had to react. Pow! She punched his ass right in his face. He ate that shit and went right for her throat. He didn't quite choke her but he had a firm enough grip to scare the shit out of her.

"Look Talia. I'm not for your crazy shit and I had no intentions on killing you, unless you want me to. Now I could fuck you up for this bullshit you pulling but I'm gone spare you. Calm the fuck down." Knight was heated at the fact that she was even acting like this.

Black Angel

Tears of anger streamed down her face as she looked him dead in his cold eyes. She saw something other than the killer that Kamari had told her that he was known to be.

"You good?" He shook her a little bit before releasing her.

"Yes."

He let her go but stayed standing in front of her staring into her eyes. It was something different about this girl but he couldn't put his finger on it. Why was she so calm? Why the fuck was she so quick to pull that gun out? In her mind she was just thinking *why me?*

Knight took her away from her thoughts when he kissed her. Talia was shocked, but at the same time excited and went along with Knight and she kissed him back. She couldn't believe she was doing this but just the thought of his aggression made her horny. Her last relationship was terrible and she was still recovering. The nigga had played like he was in love with her for two years and robbed her. But she still had plans on dealing with his ass though. All she knew now was stack or starve and kill or be killed. She showed no emotion but for some reason this nigga had her all out her hook up but she was feeling it. Then she started thinking about how he would react when she told him what type of life that she was living. The last thing she needed was for him to be in her business and judging her but if she wanted to get out of the game and have enough to survive until she found a stable job she needed to do what she needed to do and either he would respect it or not.

Tay Sheree

She wanted to make love to Knight in every room possible and to let go of some stress but she couldn't bring herself to do that just yet, she barely knew him. *Why does he have to be this damn fine? I never felt like this about a man forreal.*

Knight grabbed her gently by her slim waist, lifted her, and she automatically wrapped her legs around his strong body. He tongued her down leaving her speechless and held her there so effortlessly that it turned her on even more. They kissed passionately where they stood for at least ten minutes. The way that they were all over each other you would have thought they were long time lovers. As much as she had wanted to shoot him before she could not bring herself to do it. *Why was he so different?* If he was anyone else she would not have thought twice and shot them immediately.

She couldn't get over the fact that she was letting this man, this stranger; do her little body like this. Knight felt her knees get weak as he glided his hand up her thighs until he reached her moist place and he had to have her. He usually didn't give a fuck about these bitches out here he just ran through them and sent them about their business but this girl was something different. He had to be patient and do her body right. He carried her up to his room with her still attached to his waist looking into her eyes with every step. Their destination was the bathroom. It was gorgeous in there. The shower was big enough to hold at least 6 people comfortably. She couldn't stop staring and he proceeded because he knew that she was now comfortable with him. Knight sat her down on the ottoman and ran her

Black Angel

some bath water to the perfect temperature. He could be the perfect gentlemen when he wanted to.

Right before it was done he added a small amount of vanilla scented bubbles and spread them around in a circular motion with his hand until they blended completely with the water. She sat with her legs crossed just watching him and then the bubbles as they formed in the tub. She wasn't used to things like this so she was enjoying and savoring every bit of it. *Where has he been all of my life? I should have found him years ago. He barely knows me and he is running me bath water. But I hope he doesn't think that I forgot about those suitcases either. He gone break bread. But in the meantime i'm enjoying this. This is something that I could get used to. Long day of work and come home to dinner and a bath, yea, I would love that.*

Her thoughts were interrupted by Knight gently grabbing her hand and leading her to her bath. She appreciated the bath but she really wanted to see what that shower felt like. It looked like it could put her straight to sleep and sleep was definitely what she needed at this point and he knew it. Even though Knight was not fully sure of her occupation he sensed that she was wore out physically and mentally.

He stood Talia in front of him so that he could briefly massage her shoulders. She just stood there with her head back and eyes rolling as she let out light moans. This man really knew how to work his hands. He slowly and gently removed her clothes then laid them neatly on top of the hamper. After undressing her many thoughts raced through his head but the last thing that he wanted to do was rush in to something with her. He dabbed his hand in the water to test the temperature for her and it was just right. Knight guided Talia up on the step stool and into the tub. She let out a slight moan because the water felt so good. He turned on the massaging heads in the tub for her then went to retrieve some towels and toiletries for her. As she waited for him she unraveled her pony tail then pinned her hair natural, shoulder length up.

He came back in the bathroom and dimmed the lights. With the towels and a rag in hand he came and sat right next to her on the stool. She was sitting there looking so peaceful and relaxing that he didn't want to bother her. After startling her by touching her shoulder he lathered the rag with soap and water to wash her back. She sat up allowing him access to do so. He washed her body from head to toe not neglecting one area. He had her rinse off then he helped her out of the tub and onto one of the towels. Knight lightly towel dried her sensitive skin then rubbed her down with baby oil.

As he slid his strong hands up and down her thighs she imagined so many naughty thoughts. She felt herself getting real wet and she attempted to pull away. He nonchalantly pulled her body back toward him and continued to rub her back. When he reached behind him to grab a shirt, taking his hands off of her she let out a deep sigh because she would have exploded if he touched her a second longer. He slid the t shirt over her head then led her to his bed.

Though her pretty area was screaming for sex her body was screaming for sleep so she gave in and balled her

Black Angel

knees to her chest. Before she knew it she dozed off into a deep sleep. His bed was so comfortable that she could not fight her sleep if she wanted to.

After Talia was sound asleep he remembered that Ronnelle had texted him earlier but his mind was definitely not on her right now. Ms. Talia Marie was his main focus at this point. It was something about her and he would sit there all night to figure out what it was if he had to.

Knight wasn't ready to get out of the streets yet but this girl had him thinking that he might be ready to settle down and better himself. Knight was willing to change a lot for his Mrs. Perfect and she seemed to be it. He didn't want to sound too thirsty or anxious but he needed her to know sooner than later. He planned to tell her the truth about everything and whatever she wanted to know and he was surprised that she hadn't asked him any questions yet. Talia, on the other hand had no intentions on telling him much of anything unless he asked then she would still only "think" about it. He liked this about her and that was even more reason to give her the world. He knew that she deserved it.

He wasn't fully acquainted with Talia yet but his heart told him that she could be the one. Knight was used to being that nonchalant guy who didn't really care to have girlfriends and only held on because they did and it didn't matter to him who found out. He would leave bitches hanging high and dry but show up days later and things would still be okay between them so hey, why not do them bad. He was tired of these females who let him run over them and whom he could get whatever he wanted out of. It

Jay Sheree

was time for a change. He needed a challenge, someone who could make him chase and worry. He never met his match so he continued to fuck around with them fuck arounds. All of the bitches from around the way were too ratchet and wanna be high class for him. Knight wanted a woman. The qualities of his perfect woman were: loyalty, respect, hardworking, good looking, intelligent, independent, horny, and down to ride. One thing that he did know is that he couldn't and wouldn't wife a bitch who couldn't fuck. Shit, who would? If that bitch wasn't busting it open for a King every time that he stepped in the door then he did not want or need her.

Knight sat there for an hour texting Lalo about the crazy shit that happened to him tonight and let him know that he had to meet up with him. He also told him to do a little background check on Talia so he could see who he was dealing with. She was laying there in the bed with her back to him just thinking about all of the what ifs. Her mind was going and it was bothering her so she couldn't sleep. Not to mention that Knight was sitting up texting someone while she was laying there. All she knew was that she felt safe there and that was all that mattered.

The curiosity was killing her. All she could dream about was having relations with Knight. She tossed and turned for a while then tried to go back to sleep but for some reason she couldn't. She was woke out of her sleep by the irritating sound of Knight's phone going off from text messages. That fact that he was even texting in bed was aggravating her. But she had to have Knight and she had to have him now so she decided to try something to get his

Black Angel

attention. She got out of bed then walked around to his side and just stood there but he didn't respond to that so she took it a bit further. She pulled the XL t shirt over her head then let it fall to the ground, exposing her body. Her chocolate skin was still glistening from the baby oil that he had rubbed on her.

She let down her hair and let it fall on her shoulders. Knight had a fetish for natural hair so she had his attention now. Her 36 C's sat perfectly on her chest and she played with one of her nipples while one hand stayed in her hair. He watched her periodically while casually still texting on his phone. She played along. She had an idea that he wouldn't be able to ignore so she walked over to grab one of his desk chairs. He watched her every step as she sashayed across the room with her toned legs and ass. She sat down directly in front of him and spread her legs apart in the air as wide as she could. He loved a tease and admired her strong legs as they stayed in the air. She reached between them and began to play with her clit with her manicured fingers and she instantly began to drip. His dick rose through his pajamas and she smiled at him.

Knight had enough of her playing with herself so he got up and pulled her onto his lap. He grabbed each one of her fingers and sucked her juices off of them. Her body quivered and her head leaned back in ecstasy. He grabbed the back of her neck and passionately licked on it then he made his way to her breast. Talia was in bliss and couldn't take it anymore. He flipped her over and laid her down on her back so she could enjoy his show now. He stood in front of her removing his shirt revealing his stunning abs.

Tay Sheree

Those arms on him were gorgeous. They were so strong, so muscular. By looking at his chest you could tell that he worked out on the daily. Then off came his pants. Talia instantly fell in love. Knight was bowlegged and blessed in between his legs. She started dripping down her legs because of her fixation for bow legs.

Her body was begging for him. He stared into her eyes as he proceeded to remove his boxers. He wanted to see the expression on her face when he revealed himself to her. Her eyes widened as much as they could and he smiled. The way his body was cut from neck to ankle was beautiful and he knew it. Knight never neglected any part of his body when working out. All of his clothes were off now but he still was not ready to enter her yet. He took his time with her. From her small waist to her solid thighs he just wanted to eat her up.

Gently opening her legs he parted them one by one to get a better view of her mound. He parted her lips and using only his tongue he played with her clit. She twitched and moaned, damn near jumping off of the bed. Using his strong ass hands he clenched her ass cheeks and pulled her toward his face. She could no longer run from him. She reached and reached for everything that was not there. That shit turned him on even more to see her like that. He licked and sucked a bit harder until she came for him. He stood up and watched her pant as he was reaching in his nightstand for a condom. Knight opened the pack to the Trojan magnum XL then slid it on. He looked her in her eyes again and he knew that she was begging for him.

Black Angel

Talia couldn't take anymore waiting because she wanted him so badly. She wanted him, all of him. Her body tried to resist but it was no more faking or hiding it no matter how much she wanted to. Talia no longer cared what Knight or anyone else would think of her because the feeling was too good so she took her chances. Something came over her and she pulled Knight on top of her and kissed him. He grabbed the back of her head and stuck his tongue damn near down her throat. She followed his tongue with her own. So into kissing him Talia hadn't even noticed that Knight had parted her legs. He entered her so smooth that all she could do was bite his bottom lip. His thick ass 9" dick felt like it had reached her stomach. By starting off slow grinding he got her comfortable. With every stroke she jerked. He knew Talia was ready when she started grinding with him. She moved her hips with him to ease up the pain and clenched her muscles as tight as she could. Knight was groaning and moaning in her ear and that got her even wetter.

She put her palm on the middle of his chest to get his attention.

"Stop moving." She used her most seductive voice.

He did just that.

She grinded on him at a slow pace then a fast pace, making her own rhythm without even letting him slip out. He was in love. She wasn't finished yet.

"Turn me around." He did just that.

He flipped her over then he put his hands behind his head and watched her work. She backed all the way up on him until he could feel her flesh on his pelvis. Her body

Tay Shereé

trembled causing her muscles to get a death grip on his dick. Knight damn near collapsed on her. She was feeling real confident in her skills so he had to see if she was really about that life.

Putting his hands close together right above her ass he pushed her back down until her breast were flat on the bed. He left one hand there and put the other on the back of her neck. He had her in his favorite position where running was not an option. His roughness was tripping her out. The bed was soaked now. He moved slow paying attention to her reactions until he found her spot.

"Ooh yes! There it is!" She was hollering.

Knight smacked her ass, pulled on her hair, and bit her shoulders while fucking her. He was going so hard and she was about to explode.

"Oh my goodness. I'm coming." She could not hold on any longer.

He kept tapping the head of his penis on her G spot until she came. Then he followed.

They both washed up and headed back to bed. Then while his sleeping beauty slept he went downstairs and grabbed the suitcases. He had no intentions on hiding the contents from her, especially not after that episode they had earlier that night. She was not a hard sleeper so she laid there until she figured out what the fuck was going on. Knight came back in with the suitcases that they got from the lick. He sat in the back of the room and cut on a little lamp and went through the shit.

In one suitcase was 10 bricks. In the other was a few guns and 80 racks. "Jackpot" he said as he went over to

Black Angel

wake Talia. She walked over to the desk with him and looked at what he had counted up. They both admired the product and money.

"Wow!" Dumb fucks." She picked up a stack of money.

"So how you wanna do this? Split it in half?"

"I like how you think." She smiled and walked away.

Talia laid back down and went back to sleep. Knight continued to sit at his desk and split the cash up evenly between the two of them. He gave her the street value to make up the difference from the drugs and gave her cash from his personal stash. He planned on making some moves with the drugs himself, He had to be careful how he made his moves though since the drugs were hot. The key was to be patient and humble, he already had the skills.

Chapter Five

The sun was so bright that morning that it woke Talia out of her sleep. When she opened her eyes she immediately squinted because she had a slight headache from drinking last night. When she went to get out of bed she noticed that Knight was not in there but there was a note that had her name written neatly on it. *What could this be about?* She rolled over and opened it.

Ms. Talia Marie,
When you awake there are a few outfits in the bathroom for you to choose from. They're not recycled. I went shopping for you while you slept. I did not want to awake you. Please shower then come down to join me for breakfast.
p.s. You are very beautiful when you sleep ;)

Knight!

Talia smiled from ear to ear and headed straight to the bathroom to freshen up. She was really excited because she got to try out that gorgeous shower. As she removed her clothes in the mirror and admired her body she noticed another note lying on the counter. *This dude is nuts.* She smiled and shook her head.

Beautiful,
My intentions are good know that so don't try anything crazy when you come downstairs. This time I'll have something for yo ass. Lol

Tay Sheree

Knight!

She did not plan on acting up this time but she would still be cautious. She couldn't believe it though. This nigga was being too friendly and she hated that she liked it so much but the same time she could not deny the feeling. Nobody would ever catch her slipping again so she made sure her 19 was on the side of the bed in her purse for precautionary purposes. Yea, she heard about him but in reality she didn't know him personally so she damn sure couldn't trust him yet. She was curious to see what he was really about.

After twenty minutes of showering, Talia stepped out and dried off then headed in the room to get dressed. Sitting on the couch was a Guess and a BeBe bag. Talia was shocked because this man had taste. It's one thing to dress a man but for him to be able to dress a woman too was a big turn on. The first thing that she pulled out was an all black jogging suit and a white belly shirt with the BeBe logo on the front and she was satisfied. Today was a chill day for her and plus she had moves to make before and after her interview at 2:30p.m. so she wanted to be comfortable.

In the bottom of the bag was a pair of size 5.5 all white 90 Air Maxes, her favorite. *How did he know my sizes?* She thought as she stood in the 8ft body mirror and checked out her new fit. She loved it and was ready to go downstairs and thank Knight for it. She felt naked though. She was missing jewelry. Just then she noticed a small red bag on the floor by the mirror. *You have to be kidding me.* She

Black Angel

picked up the bag and she removed the two small boxes from the bag. One contained a Trinity heart necklace by Cartier and the other one was some original CC logo Chanel ear rings. These would now be her favorites. She owned a pair before but those were gone too. She now had a new pair to replace her old ones. After her ex took all her shit she never went to buy any new ones. Pulling her long hair back into a neat ponytail was one of the last things that she had to do. She was looking fly as hell and definitely feeling herself. One final thing that she wouldn't dare forget was perfume. She could handle that. She reached in her purse and grabbed her Viva La Juicy by Juicy Couture, she sprayed herself then she was complete.

As she walked down the stairs she smelled a mixture of cinnamon and bacon but it blended together so well. She needed a man that could cook so she wouldn't have to do it herself all of the time. Once she reached the kitchen she saw Knight standing there with an all white v neck and some Nike basketball shorts standing over the stove making homemade French toast in his stainless steel skillets. Talia stood there watching him for about a minute just staring at his body as she leaned on the wall in the doorway. What turned her on the most were his bow legs. You know what they say about men with bow legs and yes, he lived up to that.

He felt her eyes watching him and simply said
"Hello beautiful. How did you like your outfits?" He was very confident knowing that she loved every one.

If Knight didn't know anything he knew clothes. Though he wasn't a flashy nigga he could put anybody together on the fashion side.

"Why don't you just look at me?" She stood in his view and spun around to let him get a good look at her.

"Perfect." That was all he had to say because he knew it would upset her a little but not enough to make her mad. Her pouting lips were beyond sexy to him.

Within the next five minutes their plates were set up on the table and he was reaching out for her hand. *What is this about?* She thought as she placed her hand in his then bowed her head for the prayer. She was so thrown off by his gesture that she didn't even hear what he had prayed about. Never did he seem like the type to pray but she respected it to the fullest extent. Her thoughts came to a halt when Knight said amen. She repeated then proceeded to eat her food. It was so good that they did not speak again until they were finished.

"That was great!" Talia said breaking their silence after eating her meal.

"Thank you. I try. I can't be living here all alone and can't cook."

"You don't have a maid?" She asked curiously with a confused look on her face, scrunching her eyebrows. His house was so big and she wondered how he kept it up.

"Naw sweetie. The less people in my business the less problems I have on my hands. Plus I have two hands of my own so why pay someone for what I can do myself."

"Again. I really like how you think. I never cared for people doing things for me that I can do myself either."

Black Angel

They sat and talked for about an hour more before they both needed to leave to make their moves. Talia had to go get ready for her interview and Knight had to go hit the streets to make some money. What she did during her free time was on his mind heavy and he was not good with holding stuff in so he just flat out asked her.

"So Ma, what do you do for a living?"

"Well, I hustle and I do hair."

"So, doing hair is your hustle?" He had to repeat it because he thought he had heard her wrong.

"No, I hustle; sell drugs, some of that. Same shit you do. Why you surprised?" She was still sipping her orange juice through her straw, barely making eye contact with him.

"Man what! This shit is crazy. Is that why you was so quick to pull yo shit out on me? So, you about this life huh?" He smiled.

"A little more than you may know." She winked at him.

She got up from her seat and put her dishes away. He had to be smart about how he treated her now. This girl may know some shit. He left it at that because now he had to really find out who this girl was. He also had to be careful with this new product that he came up on too. He had a plan.

"So, shorty. Where you from? He needed a little more info about her."

"13513 South Parkway Drive. 131st born and raised baby."

"Ya'll getting money over there, huh?" Knight had to laugh at himself.

"I said that's where I am from, not where I trap. I might be getting it in in yo hood. You'd never know." She had to come back for that low blow that he tried to throw at her and her hood.

Their convo was real intense. Both of them felt strongly about their hood`.

"Change of subject. What do you like to do?" He didn't want any tension between them.

"Alot actually. I am very versatile and open to new ideas. I read alot and I like to dance. Whenever I have free time I workout to stay in shape or to just relieve tension you know.

"That's cool. I work out too. Can you tell?" He flexed his muscles for her while she pretended not to really care. Besides that the streets take up my time. I ain't got time for no time off."

"Ha ha. Very clever." She laughed at his sense of humor.

They cleared off the table and Talia headed out to get prepared for her interview.

Talia kissed him on his cheek before she proceeded to leave and he handed her an envelope with her half of the money because he knew that she woul soon be asking about it. She smiled and walked out the door. She was about to go shop her ass off and he was about to go do some research on this mysterious girl. She was full of surprises but he was down for a challenge.

Black Angel

Chapter Six

Yo Gotti Standing in the Kitchen played through Talia's Galaxy S III as she sat outside of the The Boys and Girls Club on 131st street so she could make her last drop of the day. She had just left her interview and it had gone well so she was hoping this would be her last drop that she would ever have to make.

"Hello." She answered her phone while still scoping the scene.

"What up fool?" Her best friend Navy yelled as if he hadn't talked to her in years.

"Shit, making moves bout to go to Nikki house. What you up to?"

"Man, tell Nikki I said what's up with them buns! I'm chilling though bout to head to the Y to work out and play basketball. The bitches love a nigga who play ball." He was laughing as loud as he could into her phone.

They joked back and forth as usual.

"Nigga you so fucking lame."

Talia and Navy had been friends since 5th grade at Cranwood Elementary and haven't parted since. He was her heartbeat. Yea, she loved her 2 female friends but they could never amount to Navy. He knew her deepest and darkest secrets and she knew his. Nobody could break their bond and they planned on taking their secrets to the grave. He came too real and they clicked from the jump. All of their exes hated their relationship but far as they were concerned they didn't need anyone else because they held each other down to the fullest.

Tay Sheree

"Navy dude, I have something to tell you but right now ain't a good time. I have to go home and change out of these clothes." She stopped the laughter and got serious.

"When and where can you meet me?"

"The usual at 7:30 p.m."

She knew exactly where to meet him, which was at Blue Point Grille on the corner of W.6th and St. Clair where they both loved to eat. Simple things always made the both of them happy but seafood made her even more happy. She loved her best friend.

It was 7:42 and Navy was late as usual. She didn't mind because she was used to it and besides her and Knight had been texting all day and talking on the phone every chance that they had got. Navy pulled up next to her in his Escalade EXT straight flexing. That fool lived for fancy cars. Talia settled for her 2011 Impala today which was a nice car but he always took it overboard. She hopped out dancing to Jeezy's song Damn Lie as it played loud through all of Navy's speakers in his truck then she walked over and punched him in his forearm.

"Yo bitch ass always late"! She yelled in a playful voice.

"I had to drop off Martin at his mother house." Martin is Navy's only son. He was born to one of Navy's many girlfriends.

Their table was ready because Talia called in advance to reserve their special spot so when they arrived they would be directed to their seats.

"So, I met this guy." Talia started talking but Navy interrupted her with his childishness.

Black Angel

"GUY! Girl please." He was cracking the fuck up as if she was joking or something. She cut her eyes at him. "See what i'm saying. No, seriously. I met this guy named Knight at the bar and I wound up spending the night at his house." She paused then shook her head at herself because she couldn't believe what had just come out of her mouth.

"Do I need to remind you what happened with Jay?" Navy said trying to look out for Talia.

She had been single since her ex Jay had got locked up for beating her ass and killing their unborn after he had robbed her and set her up. It took her a long time to recover from that. Getting back on her feet, getting another house and more clothes was difficult. Not to mention the emotional stress that she went through after losing the baby. Later after her recovery the doctor told her that she would have had a little girl. She was heartbroken afterwards and still thinks about it.

Yea, she was still mad as fuck at him but as fucked up as it may sound she still loved him. She was writing him frequently at first too but she got out of her feelings and just stopped. Now her side nigga Cordero, she just fucked him from time to time since Jay had been gone. They kicked it too but nobody knew of them and they didn't plan on letting it be known either. Of course Navy, Nikki, and Kamari knew but that was only in case some shit popped off and he wanted to try some fuck shit.

"So, you like him huh?"

Jay Shereé

"Yea man he is cool as fuck. He bought me everything that I have on and he barely even knows me. That shit is crazy, right?"

She was smiling extra hard and her best was happy for her because he hadn't seen her this happy in a while.

"Damn! You put it on him like that!" He was trying to be funny acting like they were having girl talk. "Just be careful Li. I don't want you to get hurt." Now he was getting serious.

"I'm good Navy baby, you know I got this."

"Alright. Just be cool and pay attention Li."

He ended the conversation there because he didn't want to scare her away from the chance of her being happy again plus she is a grown ass woman and can handle herself. He knew that shit with her and Jay had her still fucked up. Shit him too. He sat there at the hospital with her every day the whole two months that she was there assisting her with her recovery and paid for her therapy on top of taking her every day. There was nothing that they would not do for each other.

"How was your day?" She tried changing the subject.

"It was chill. I need some new niggas to work out with man. These niggas don't do nothing but brag about bitches and money." He shook his head in disgust.

"I mean like whatever happened to people having real goals. One nigga, every trip be talking bout how he gotta make these trips to visit his baby mama and kid and how she is crazy as fuck. I can barely deal with Martin

Black Angel

living twenty minutes away from me let along a different city."

He continued to spill out everything to his best friend knowing that she wouldn't tell anyone else.

"He's bout his money though I give him that." They sat, ate, drank, and talked for about two hours. They cherished times like these because they really didn't have anyone but each other.

Zzzzzh......Zzzzzh. Talia's phone vibrated across the table. She wiped her fingers to get rid of the grease from her food then grabbed the phone. When she clicked on her unread email messages she opened the one with the subject that said Cleveland Clinic HR department. Her heart raced as she hesitated to open it. She mustered up the courage to press open. This message could make or break her.

"I got the job man!" She jumped out of her seat and blurted out the good news.

"That's good as fuck. I didn't wanna bring it up cuz I didn't know what happened at the interview." They both laughed out loud at his foolishness and proceeded to celebrate her success.

"Waiter! We need some fuckin' drinks!"

Chapter Seven

"Man, i'm not on this shit with you Ronnelle. Until you get the test i'm cool. I just sent you $1,200 three days ago, so if you blew that shit already then I can't help you." Knight was yelling into the phone, aggravated at the fact that Ronnelle would even call him on some fuck shit.

He had been fucking with Talia for about six months now so he really wasn't feeling Ronnelle anymore. He loved this girl til the death of him but he could no longer deal with the craziness and outrageous demands that came with her.

"Knight, that's fucked up! I told you it was only one time so why are you acting like this?" Ronnelle pleaded while crying because she was still embarrassed about the whole situation even after all the years that passed.

She had left for school and found some lame out there that she fell for and fucked then wound up pregnant. The crazy thing about it was that Knight had also hit her around the same time. She was still his bottom bitch but until he knew the truth about lil Sharod things would stay the same between them. He had been doing her so dirty that she was begging him for a paternity test but he just couldn't stomach up the strength to do it. In his mind she was already tainted so him finding out that Sharod wasn't his would take him over the top. He took care of that boy his whole life while the other nigga wasn't even anywhere to be found. The last thing Knight wanted to think about was Sharod because he was good regardless but eventually he would have to find out the truth no matter how much it could possibly hurt him.

Tay Sheree

"I have to go. I'll be out there tomorrow morning." He hung up in her face.

There wasn't much more that Knight could do to make her feel like shit but he could never trust her again and that spark that once was could never be there again. She was the reason that he started smoking and he sat in his GMC Denali and blazed the fuck up. He was geeked but he needed something else This stress shit was killing him. He went to the YMCA, which was what all Cleveland niggas called the Y, to work out. His friend Lalo was there already. Knight went straight to the weight bench where Lalo spotted him. Knight had a lot on his mind and Lalo knew it so Knight just started talking.

"Aye man! What would you do if yo bitch had a baby and she fucked another nigga?"

"Man, I might take her back after I fuck her up for cheating on me because that shit definitely ain't cool. It would all depend on if the baby turns out to be mine and how much I love her forreal. It's different for everybody. That's a fucked up situation to be in so you just have to follow your heart Knight. If you love Ronnelle hear her out." Lalo gave his honest opinion and threw Ronnelle's name in there so that Knight knew that he understood what he was talking about.

Knight already knew that Lalo knew who and what he was talking about so there was no need to say any names; he just wanted to vent.

"So, Sharod ain't yours?" Slightly confused, Lalo had to ask.

Black Angel

"See that's the thing. I don't know yet. Shit, I ain't gone lie. I'm scared to go take the test but we're going tomorrow morning. The suspense is killing me. I wouldn't know what to do if he wasn't mine. He's my heart man." Knight got so emotional just talking about it so he looked to Lalo to either say something or change the subject. He hit the weights even harder.

"I can't really say much cuz i'm not in the situation you know. All I can say is just do what you feel is best for you and lil homie. If you feel that you can forgive her then love them both sincerely and unconditionally. If not then leave her ass alone comepletely and take care of your responsibilities. And that's real."
Lalo could never lie to his best friend and that's what made their bond so strong. They had each other's backs to the grave.

"Word." Knight always said that to basically say what's understood ain't gotta be explained.

Knight had enough of that conversation so they headed to the courts. Knight stayed at the Y for a few hours then he went home, showered, and then continued to text Talia Marie. This became a daily routine for them. They kept in touch and kicked it every day unless one of them had some business to handle. Their relationship was one of a kind.

They laid in their beds talking for 6 hours straight about everything possible. They learned something new about each other every day. He just wanted to know everything about her inside and out.

"So, how is your new job going?"

"It's great I must say. I am blessed to say that I even have a job. I'm adjusting to this life that's all but I could get used to this."

They took turns asking questions and opening up about important things and events in their lives. Talia confided in him about her incident with Jay. Knight only told her bits and pieces about Ronnelle. Skeletons were being brought out without ever giving too much detail. He told her that he had a trip to L.A. to take Saturday morning so they would have to take a rain check on their date.

"I have plans for us that day. When will you be back?" Talia was getting a little because she thought that her hard work would be ruined.

"These are quick plans baby. I'll be back to spend time with you, I promise." He made sure that he kept all of his promises to her.

Chapter Eight

Talia and Knight had an irreplaceable relationship. They fought like a married couple, talked and played like best friends, and fucked like there was no tomorrow. She had even moved into his home in Shaker. Redecorating everything prior to the move was their way of making them comfortable with the new change. There wasn't a day that they were apart after the move. Only thing that separated them was business. They kept everything exciting by trying new things. Working out together, attending events, and making Sundays their designated day strictly for them was regular. They preferred to chill and lay up on their off days since every other day they were on the move.

Since Knight had found out that Talia was out there hustling he made her take self defense classes. She wasn't in the streets as much since she got the new job but he wanted her to be safe with or without him around. He knew that time to time she would dip back in the street life. It ain't as easy to get out of the game as it is to get in. They also went to the gun range every two weeks to keep their aim on point. This kept them both busy and away from the drama that came with the streets and the thirsty bitches out there that wanted them apart. Even though she was sweet and loving she had a bad side to her where she could turn into a cold hearted killer. She was his Black Angel.

While he was at the gym working out she would be at her boxing classes downstairs. Knight made sure that they both stayed in shape regardless of how they did it. His 1,200 pushups a day did his body good. He was all about him and his girl appearance. She was nowhere close to that but her body was still cold.

She was sitting on their suede Herman Miller Goetz sofa, stretched out with her oversized gray crewneck sweater and boy shorts on. It was turning him on seeing her with his knee high Nike socks stretched up her chocolate legs. He loved her tomboy style and she loved to lounge in his oversized clothes.

Within the last six months they had been doing very well in their relationship. They traveled to Mississippi to visit her grandfather's grave. They worked out together as a daily routine. Including one another in as much as possible was what they did. Thursdays was their day that they alternated weekly to cook dinner. Their relationship grew very healthy off of these things. Building off of each other instead of trying to bring the other down was the key.

"What you reading sexy?" He was trying to sound like he cared at least a little but really he just wanted her attention.

"Another one of my urban novels. May I help you?" She tried to sound annoyed knowing damn well that she had been waiting on him to come say something to her.

"Damn. I can't ask? I thought you were reading some book about deception or something like that?"

"The book is called Juicy Deception and I finished it yesterday. I told you that I have a whole collection that I am going through."

Then she was interrupted by a kiss. His aggressiveness always made her extra horny and that kiss

Black Angel

had put her on ten. She was never shy with Knight. It was like he brought out another side of her. He brought out something in her that she could not control nor did she want to. He picked her up, pinned her to the nearest wall, and then tongued her down until she begged for air. Her weakness was a good kisser and that he was.

Letting her down off of the wall he then grabbed her neck with his left hand and played with her pussy through her boy shorts with the other hand as he whispered in her ear.

"Why do always like to act up Talia? You're mine right?" He was talking to her in the most seductive voice in her ear as he licked on her earlobe and she just melted.

"Yes daddy." That was all that she managed to get out between pants.

"Well let me know it then." He laid her down right on top of her $2,000 Stepevi, 3D area rug that she was so amped to buy.

He would replace it just as easy as he bought it so he did not care what happened to it even though she would whine as usual. She was so spoiled but he loved her so much that he couldn't help but to give her what she wanted. She always returned the favor with no questions asked.

The rug was so rich in texture that you couldn't even tell that you were on the floor. He pulled her boy shorts off and exposed her pretty area. He sat there and stared at her for a minute because she was so beautiful to him. Her clit was jumping and she was feigning for Knight and he knew it. The more she begged the hornier he got. He loved to tease her because it made the sex 10x's better. He licked her

Tay Sheree

inner thighs then wasted no more time and he dived right in face first. His head game was cold enough to skip sex but she wanted all of him. He fucked her with his tongue and then she gave him some head and they came over and over. Her body was shaking uncontrollably and he was loving the sight of it! She begged him to enter her but he wasn't ready.

"Please baby, I need you." She cried out as her body trembled.

He just stared at her then he pulled out his 9" pole. Just the sight of his shit made her leak. He stroked himself in front of her and made her watch and she couldn't take it anymore so she decided to give him a little motivation. She turned over and laid her chest down low enough so that her pussy was looking him right in the face and started fingering herself. He smiled at her attempt to tease him and continued to stroke himself while watching her. He had enough of her playing with his pussy because she knew that he hated that even though it was making him rock solid. His bitch would not need to touch herself for as long as he was living.

He slid right behind her so fast that it startled her and she lost her balance. He caught her with his left arm and entered her all in one motion. She came instantly. She had been acting up and giving him attitude lately so he had to fix that, get her together and let her know that he was still the King. He smacked her ass, bit her softly on her back, and pulled her hair. She was in heaven and didn't know what to do with herself. She was pulling the carpet and

Black Angel

even her own hair. They switched positions so much that she got dizzy. She rode him like an animal. Her sex game was cold. Talia spun around on him and did the reverse cowgirl so that he could watch her ass cheeks clap as she rode him some more. She put her hands on her thighs then slowly slid then them down to her ankles. She sat there for a second so that he could admire her body in this position. Talia look back then bounced up and down to her own tempo. He was loving that shit and when he couldn't help his self he grabbed her waist and went as deep as he could, pounding Talia until he felt her body shaking. They came together and then they were both stuck on the floor for a while. He carried her into the bathroom where they bathed and brushed their teeth. He dressed her then went to bed. He always reminded her why she put up with his bullshit!

Chapter Nine

When Navy opened his eyes something didn't sit right with him. He had his best friend on his mind heavy today. The last time that he had a gut feeling like this Talia was in the hospital in critical condition from Jay. He could not quite put his finger on what was bothering him but he would figure it out.

He started his daily routine of making his homemade protein shakes then he hit up Talia.

"Best. What you in to later?" He said to her.

"Shit. No moves. I just got off work so i'm home. What's up?"

"Let's meet up later."

"Cool. Let me nap first. I'm tired as hell. Today was a rough day for me at work." Talia yawned into the phone.

"My day is rough already and I haven't even washed my ass yet. I'll tell you about it later though. I'm bout to head to the Y and get this lil work out in."

"I'ts a bet. Just hit me up." Talia hung up

Navy had so much on his mind that he did not want to think about. But before he left the house he needed to pack his suitcase for his trip to L.A. He turned on some music, zoned out, and did what he needed to do. Navy was a professional photographer and he traveled a lot to shoot for people. His biggest and most important showcase was coming up in L.A. And he was more excited than ever. He planned on surprising Talia with plane and show tickets so that she could come be by his side to support him. It was time for another get together with his best friend. They had a lot to talk about so their meeting later on would be beneficial.

When he pulled up he noticed the same man from before sitting in his truck arguing real loud on the phone with some woman. He heard every word that was being said while he grabbed his equipment out of his trunk. He was so sick of hearing this nigga whining that it was ridiculous. When he closed the trunk and turned around Knight was standing right there in his face, so close he could feel him breathing.

"What's up?" Navy said breaking the awkward silence that came with his approach. "I'm Navy." He extended his hand to dap him up.

"I'm Knight. What's good?" He gave Navy a simple head nod then started to walk in the building. Knight didn't shake niggas hands unless he really fucked with you.

"Wait. Wait. Hold up. So, you are Knight, the one that my best friend is crazy over. Small world." He was right on his heels.

"And your best friend is?" Knight didn't know what the hell he was talking about.

"Talia." He replied and Knight eased up.

"Aww. Damn that's crazy. We never got to meet man. She told me a lot about you. I heard you travel a lot. What's up with you though; you good?" Knight went on.

"I'm good you know. Just working. I have a show for some of my photography coming up soon."

Black Angel

"For real. That's what's up. Where you headed to this time?" Knight asked knowing that he really could give a fuck less but he did not want to seem too rude.

"I'm to L.A. this time. I have a surprise for Talia too. I want her to come out there with me. She has been dying to make it to one of my shows."

Knight felt like he had hit the jackpot. It had to be a coincidence that Navy's show was in L.A.

"That's what's up. I hope ya'll have fun. Good luck."

Knight hated the fact that they were so friendly with each other. He was very protective of his woman. This pretty boy motherfucka had betta not be trying anything crazy with his bitch. He figured that he would look into this showcase in L.A. and "bump into" Navy out there and straighten some things out.

"Don't tell her though. I want it to be a surprise."

"Oh naw. I ain't never been bout that snitching life. You don't have to worry bout me saying shit." He assured him because he had some other plans in mind that Talia would never find out about.

"Thanks man. I haven't seen her tough ass like this in years. Keep up the good work." Navy said sarcastically but not enough for Knight to notice.

"I will. It's crazy that we're here together damn near everyday and we never met." Knight said with his face a little twisted up.

He honestly did not believe that this whole time Navy had no clue who he was. He was lightweight ready to beat his ass but he kept it smooth and let Navy think shit was cool. Their conversation continued until they started working out and Navy couldn't take his mind off of the conversation that him and Knight had just had.

There was no way that Talia knew about all of this shit that I hear this nigga talking about. I can't let her go out like that but I am not tryna fuck up what she got going on with ol' dude. While at the same time Knight knew that Navy knew too much about him and he had to react quick, but not too quick. He had a plan.

Chapter Ten

I can't wait to throw this party. He better love me for life all of this damn money that I am spending. Talia was sitting there thinking to herself as she sat on her bed Indian style in her camo footed pajamas with her notebook in her lap planning Knight's 25th surprise birthday party. Everything would be planned to the tee. She needed it to be perfect. She had to call her partner in crime, Kamari to give her all the details then call Navy to tell him. Those were the only two people besides Nikki that she could trust with that information. As soon as she hung up with Kamari her phone started ringing, playing a part of a skit by Lil Wayne called Loyalty. *I Wanna Teach You A Little Bit About Loyalty, The Main Name Of This Game Is Respect And Loyalty.*

Navy was already calling her. Loyalty meant everything to her and their relationship was the perfect example. No crossing lines, no secrets, no crossing each other.

"What up fool. Where you at?" This was her usual greeting for him.

"I'm at the house chilling. We need to meet up asap!"

"Shit, meet me at Cold Stone in 30. I had some shit to talk about with you anyways." She was sliding out of her one piece as she spoke.

"Bet."

Surprisingly, Navy wasn't late today. He pulled in and hopped out faster than she had ever seen him do before because he had a few things to get off of his chest. They walked in together and began their convo.

"What's on your mind best?" Talia started.

"What do you want first? The good news or the bad news?"

"Let's start with the good. Don't fuck up my mood just yet." She burst out laughing.

"Alright then. Man, i'm so excited. I got the gig in L.A.!"

"Oh my God boo, that's great! When do you leave?"

"My flight is booked for Saturday. I can't wait to go do my thang." Navy stopped talking because Talia didn't look too enthused. "What's wrong? I thought you were excited for me?"

"I am." She said dryly.

"You didn't let me tell you the best part though Li. I got two seats and tickets to the show. I want you to come with me!" He tried to keep explaining to her hoping that her expressions would change.

"Navy I can't." She said pouting her perfect lips. "That's the day of Knight's surprise party that I am planning and I wanted to invite you." She tried to tell Navy but he wasn't really trying to hear it.

They both sat there heartbroken and didn't really have anything else to say to each other. They ordered their ice cream and sat back down. Talia decided to break the silence with simple conversation.

"So are you mad at me?"

He hit her with the stale face. "Nope."

She knew that he was really upset with her but it's not like she knew and could have avoided this. She kept trying.

Black Angel

"Best friend, come on now! Don't be like that. How could I have known? You know I would give anything to be there for you, you're my fucking best friend!" She was yelling now and drawing attention to them.

"Exactly, so you should be there for me!"

"Wow! Really? Just one time I can't make it and you're tripping? Un-fucking-believeable."

"Right. Cuz you would rather party with a no good nigga that's playing yo dumb ass." Navy finally boldly spit out that other thing that he needed to talk about.

Talia bust out in tears. No one else's words seemed to faze her except her grandmother, Navy's, and now Knight's.

"You know that's real fucked up. You know how much I care for the both of you and I would kill to be there with you. I wish I could be at both places at the same time. But for one time in my life I am happy and you try to take that from me." She just got up, pushing her chair back very hard causing it to rock and walked out.

He was so upset with her that he didn't even chase her while she was so upset that she didn't look back. She couldn't believe that Navy, her best friend out of all people would say such hurtful things to her. She was there through thick and thin but as soon as she finds happiness someone always tries to take that from her. Her heart was broken. Choosing between her man and best friend was the last thing that she wanted to do. She couldn't and she damn sure wouldn't. Where's the loyalty in that? Both of them would be happy somehow. She had to make that happen.

Tay Shereé

There was no way to rebook the party because the halls were reserved. Navy could not reschedule his showcase either because the date was pre set. This was a really hard decision for her to make that she wished never had to be made. She sat there and thought long and hard as she drove away about what she could possibly do to satisfy Navy. She knew they wouldn't be mad at each other for long. They had petty arguments all of the time but for some reason she felt like this time it would be different. It finally came to her and she decided that she was going to set up a showcase here in Cleveland for him when he decided to get over his attitude. He should have already known that it would come a time when they would go their separate ways with different people. That didn't mean that their friendship had to end and she was afraid that Navy wouldn't understand that. He would love that. He did work everywhere but in his hometown. It was time for him to represent for The Land!

Chapter Eleven

Strippers. Check. Chocolate Fountain. Check. Bartenders. Check. Dancing cages. Check. Surprise gift. Check. Talia had everything perfectly planned out and she was so excited. Knight was very picky but she knew that he would love and appreciate this, especially when no one ever really does anything for him. It was still so much to do with so little time and Talia was oh so determined to do it. Knight was her man and she was going to give him the best birthday party ever. All she knew is when her birthday came around he had better put some wild shit together for her as she did for him. As she walked through the mall with her girls looking for the perfect jewelry so many thoughts went through her head. They had already finished their shopping without her because she was working alot of overtime but she wanted them there with her while she finished hers. They made it a girl's day out since they barely got to see each other anymore because of their conflicting schedules. She thought about her last encounter with her best friend and she got upset all over again. She couldn't believe he would say some foul shit like that to her. She shook that shit off and got back to business.

Once they stepped in Sak's she snapped back.

"Hi! How are you?" The clerk asked the group of beautiful women.

"We are good and you?" Talia spoke for them all.

"Are you looking for anything specific?"

"Why yes I am. First, I need to find the perfect necklace to go with a black Valentino bow back strapless jumpsuit."

Tay Sheree

Her and Knight would be matching tonight. Once he made it back from his trip she would present his outfit to him as a gift then would pretend that they were going to a big birthday dinner. Her plan and everything was flawless. The clerk was impressed by Talia's taste in designer.

"Well, we have this selection over here where your options are limitless." She directed Talia over to the classier jewelry.

"Oooh nice." She fingered through a long row of necklaces until she found one that stood out.

"What do ya'll think about this?" She modeled the jewelry for Kamari, Nikki, and the clerk.

"That's hot girl!" Nikki complimented her friend.

"Hell yea! That's the one." Kamari told her.

"Yea. I'm feeling this one." She posed in the mirror picturing her outfit.

"I'll take this one." She followed the clerk up to the register and purchased the long silver knotted necklace that would drape perfectly over her jumpsuit. She was carrying so many bags and she was just ready to go sit down. It was almost time to pick up Knight from the airport and she needed a nap. She smiled at how fly they would be tonight. The last thing that she had to do was pick Knight up a pair of Diamond stud silver back ear rings to match their watches. Their matching Audimar Piguet's came in the mail earlier that day. She locked them up in their jewelry safe before she left. They were worth too much to just let get stolen.

They always killed it when they stepped out. Her shopping and their outfits were now complete.

Black Angel

"Okay ya'll let's go over the plans." Talia started talking to her friends as they headed out to their cars.

"Kamari, you are in charge of the strippers with your bi curious ass." She laughed out loud then continued with business. "I got twelve of them so i'll give you their contact information so that you can set up a routine with them.

"And you Nikki will be in charge of my finances. That means collecting my entry fees and being in control of the money that we will be throwing on the strippers."

"Got it?" She looked at both of them and raised her eye brow on some boss shit.

"Yep!" They were ready to party.

Before Talia pulled off she emailed both of her friends well written out plans of how things would go. After everything was read and understood everything should run smooth.

Chapter Twelve

Knight was looking real suspicious out here and Talia would find out what he was really about sooner than later. Navy thought to himself. He saw Knight riding past a diner where he went to eat before the showcase and he followed him. He had to move quick so he could make it on time for his show so he planned to snap a few pictures and keep it moving. As he was about to pull off he thought that Knight had spotted him so he turned his head and pulled off. He was in a rental with slightly tinted windows so it would not be that easy to decipher who he was anyways, so he had thought.

This fuck nigga Knight really out here tryna play Talia. Navy thought to himself as he looked through the pictures that he took of Knight and Ronnelle out in public in L.A. They even had a little boy with them. Navy went straight to Walgreens and printed them out. He put them right in a manilla envelope and addressed it to Talia. Since she didn't want to believe him he had to do better and show her. He knew some bullshit was gone pop off once he got back to the land but he didn't care. As long as Talia knew the truth and was happy he was cool with whatever else came his way.

֍֍֍֍֍֍

The night was approaching and Knight was ready to get back home to his girl. He grew restless from sitting at the airport for an hour waiting on his plane to depart. He knew he should have never gone back out there to see

Tay Sheree

Ronnelle and he was pretty damn mad that he had seen Navy out there. But his plan was already in place and Navy would never make it back to Cleveland. He was tired of lying to Talia and the last thing that he needed was her "best friend" throwing salt on his game! He would soon get to the bottom of that best friend too even though it didn't matter anymore. He wasn't for that shit and Talia should've already known that. He was just glad that he had got that DNA test over.

  He went out there to L.A. and Ronnelle was showing her ass. Even though he still loved her and Sharod she crossed him and he knew that they could never come back from that. He only went out there to clear things up with her and make sure that they had a clear understanding on things and what would happen after the results were back. He went and picked her and Sharod up and headed to the clinic to take the test. Sharod was asking all types of questions that he did not know how to answer and that pissed him off even more.

  Knight sent for somebody to meet him out there on a separate flight to handle Navy for him and the unexpected happened. When he was leaving Ronnelle's house he caught Navy spying on him so his people had to act quick. Knight couldn't risk Navy making it back to Cleveland to tell Talia anything mixing up stories, telling shit that he has no clue about. He couldn't chance how many times that Navy had spotted him making these trips to see Ronnelle. He was already in too deep and that's why his plan was already in place. Navy would never make it back to Cleveland. He knew once he had received that call

Black Angel

when he got back on the plane that the plan had been executed.

As the plane departed he got lost in his thoughts. He had already popped a Xanax too to calm his nerves. As much as he traveled you would think he would be used to this shit. His birthday dinner was in 6 hours and he had big plans this year. A lot would change for the better. Talia had planned a dinner for them once he touched down and he decided to propose to her during that time. The most important thing was giving her the family that she always dreamed of. He was only getting older and he wanted to spend the rest of his life with this girl. Her ambition alone was sexy along with that slim body of hers that he couldn't resist. He could not wait to get his birthday sex. Just thinking about her on top of him made him grin all silly to himself in public. Knight couldn't keep his hands off of her. Before he knew it he dosed off. The rest of the flight he dreamed about his future with Talia. They had their share of ups and downs but it was time for him to stop playing games with her. Only thing standing in his way was himself.

The flight was finally over and when he landed Talia was right there to pick him up. As soon as she spotted him she hopped out the car and ran full speed straight to him. He sat his bags down and embraced her with a hug. She pulled herself as close to him as she could to get a whiff of his Creed cologne. She was so addicted to his scent. No matter how long they were apart they acted as if they had gone years without seeing each other.

Tay Sheree

"Baby i'm so glad you're back." She whispered in his ear.

"I'm glad to be back here with you."

They stayed there for about three minutes talking and hugging then they hopped in the car. He wanted to drop down and propose to her then and there but he decided to wait. He didn't want to spoil the moment.

Their house was looking and smelling fresh for Knight when he came home and he was impressed by his woman. She always knew how to keep him happy. House stayed clean, dick stayed pleased, and her conversation was always on point. One thing that he hated was a bum bitch that could only stimulate his dick and not his mind and that she was far from. He opened the bedroom door to find an outfit laid out across the bed for him. His bitch had taste. The colors for the night were black, red, and silver. She had him wearing a black Armani fitted shirt with the matching slacks and some Tom Ford loafers to go along with it. Right next to his clothes was her outfit and he was so ready for her to put it on. She would be wearing her all black Valentino bow back strapless jumpsuit with a red Chanel clutch and some red Christian Louboutin platform pumps. Their outfits always coordinated and he loved that. His and hers.....he loved the sound of that.

He hopped in the shower to get freshened up so they could make their reservations. As he closed his eyes and leaned his head back under the water letting the sounds take him away he felt Talia's small hand on his chest. Knight grinned because he knew that sooner or later she would creep in like she always did. Her soft hands glided up and down his chest then she continued down to his manhood. He was already rock solid from the light kisses that she was planting on his back. She stood directly in front of him and began to plant more kisses on his chest. Talia had a fetish for muscular bodies and Knight took the cake.

After a short while she found herself working her way down until she made it to her destination. She squatted down until her mouth met his piece then she slowly put his dick in her mouth. Knight let out a slight moan. She started slowly bobbing her head back and forth, and back and forth until he started reaching everywhere. But he knew her rules, if he touched her head she would stop. She knew how to control her own head. His signs of struggle made her bob harder. She was an animal! She gripped his balls while still sucking and he damn near jumped out of his skin. Knight was damn near climbing the shower wall.

The intensity of the shower water flowing out of both massaging shower heads, from both directions and Talia trying to take him out was ridiculous. She felt his body jerk and that was her cue to go ham but he had other plans for her. He lifted Talia right off of her feet, turned her around, and bent her right the fuck over like the boss that he was. She loved when he was aggressive and he knew it. He slowly entered her and they both gasped in unison. Her juice box was so warm and tight but what was best was that he knew that he had her to himself.

He started off slow with his strokes then after about the 5th one he started straight dogging her how he knew that she loved it. Talia was trying to run but those arms, man those arms had a good ass grip on her waist. That running shit turned him on even more. He grabbed her hips and threw her back and forth on his dick as hard as he could. He had a lot on his mind and what better way to release stress than to let it out during sex. Either she really missed him or she was just doing those damn kegels again because her pussy was extra good and tight today. He tried to hold on as long as he could but her shit was feeling too right. He exploded right inside of her and she came right along with him. Her legs got weak and she went to collapse but he quickly grabbed her, turned her around, and tounge kissed her. This night was so intense for the both of them.

  He washed both his and her body then they got out and got dressed. Talia always liked to get dressed in the guest room because Knight was always listening to some Jay-Z no matter the occasion and she preferred club bangers or simple slow music. Slow was her favorite but a little liquor in her system as she dressed always changed her mood. Every once in a while you would catch her in a ratchet mood and today was one of those days. She was definitely feeling herself after that shower with Knight. Images kept replaying in her head and she couldn't wait for round two after the party.

Chapter Thirteen

They pulled up to the Mediterranean hall in Bedford Heights and there were cars everywhere. Talia wanted to bust out and say surprise herself but she had to keep her cool and not ruin it. She had arranged for valet to be at the door waiting for them to get out. Knight had never been to this place before so he was hoping that their food was good seeing how they had just worked up an appetite. They got out and the two doors of the building opened up and a camera man came out.

"Say cheese Bae!" She told Knight right as the camera man started snapping pictures.

He wasn't really into pictures but it was his birthday plus he knew not to piss Talia off so he went along with it. He stood behind her and hugged her waist. Then they switched up and she kissed his cheek. That camera kept rolling and it definitely loved them because they complimented each other so well. She was loving every moment of this. Talia and the love of her life were creating great memories with hopefully more to come in the future. They were one fly ass couple.

Both of the doors opened and they were ushered inside. There was one small table set up in the middle of the floor made for two. There were no plates though just two wine glasses filled with Dom Perignon, his favorite, and a candle burning. As they sat down they were instructed to read what looked like menus. When Knight opened his it read *Happy Birthday Baby!!! I love you! I know you are tired of all of these tricks so go wash your hands and our dinner will be served. Love always, Your Talia Marie.* He wanted to be agitated but he couldn't because he couldn't lie, she had him on his toes but he was very impatient and ready to eat.

By the time that he looked up Talia was already disappearing to the ladies room. It was not a ladies room though. It was her entrance to the back of the party. She laid that bitch out so that he would never see it coming. He walked to the door to what he thought was the mens restroom then once he opened up the door all he heard was "Surprise" from so many voices around the room. Lalo was right in front to dap him up and hand him his birthday gift personally. Talia was right next to him with Kamari and Nikki. The whole crew was looking fly as hell. They were all a part of the plan and they played their parts well.

"Happy birthday big head!" Nikki gave him a big hug.

"How does it feel knowing you pushing thirty?" Kamari followed with her hug.

"Thanks ya'll. I feel great to be alive. That's it. I'm blessed."

Knight was fasho surprised and happy as hell. His lady did one hell of a job putting this event together. He knew it was all a little fishy when for one the reservations were for 9:30pm and it was now 10:30pm then the damn table didn't have any plates. He forgot that he was even hungry when he began walking around. He needed to see how cold his bitch was at putting his shit together. She really out did herself. He embraced her with a huge hug and a kiss. Now he was really proud that he was making this choice to make her his wife, especially on this day. It was perfect timing. She was so happy seeing a smile on his face. It was priceless. His cake was a suitcase with money falling out of it and it said "The world is ours." On the stage there was a huge box in the shape of a present that looked big enough to fit 12 people and he was so anxious to see what was in there. Cages hung from the ceiling with the party guest dancing in them and the bartenders were sexy as hell making special drinks for everyone with no ticket. The tab was on Talia tonight. After everyone finished eating at the huge buffet it was time to party. The building was full of black people so you already know they were packing plates more than they were eating them. Talia didn't care though because they don't do leftovers in her household.

Just then the music got louder and Two Chainz birthday song came on. A boom was heard across the whole party and the big present box opened. Talia made sure that Knight and Lalo were standing right in front when it happened because they were getting first dibs on whichever big booty bitch that they wanted. Out came 12 big booty strippers. Knight, Lalo and Talia were front and center. Nikki walked up with her big booty and started mocking the strippers.

"Get yo ass up there too and make me some money." Talia yelled to her bestfriend.

Kamari grabbed Talia and Nikki's hand to come on stage with her but Talia respectfully declined. The two of them hopped on stage and acted a fool. Security attempted to get them down but Talia had to assure them that it was

Tay Shereé

cool and that she approved of it. Kamari's ass was up there getting acquainted with Peaches, one of the strippers.

"Get it girls!" Talia was yelling from the crowd throwing money on the stage having fun, showing out for her man.

Since Nikki's role was to handle all of the finances from the party she handed the three of them a sack of dollar bills. Each bag contained 1000 singles. The invitations strictly stated that you needed at least 100 singles to get in and if you could not comply then Talia was personally coming to the door to suggest that you boss yo life up and leave. Straight like that! And anyone that knew her knew she would bar none. There was even a machine at the door for those who would claim to not have change. If Talia respected anyone it was someone who is about their money and she would make sure that these ladies were well paid tonight. Talia had put too much time and effort in to this party so please believe that you had to pay to get in and security was tight. There was also a V.I.P. List at the door. If you were V.I.P. You got to go in the back and get private dances with complimentary drinks. Knight would find out about that after the party that she had a personal after party planned for the two of them at their new house that she had purchased. She had been saving up money before Knight had even entered her life. Her man deserved the best and that's exactly what he would get even if she had to spend her last. Little did she know he had a surprise of his own.

All of the strippers got to do solos and make some individual money while the dance floor was still available.

Black Angel

The whole party was shaking. Talia was so ecstatic that she pulled this off. He also admired how organized that she was. She kept both of them in order. Then the DJ gave everyone a break and turned on a slow song. Poetic justice by Kendrick Lamar played and Talia got real excited, this was her favorite song right now. She grabbed her man and headed to the floor. For the whole song they goofed around and danced. After the song went off Knight interrupted the DJ and asked for the mic.

"Aye! Lalo. Come here real quick." He called for his brother. He whispered in his ear then went back to what he was doing. He couldn't leave his nigga in the dark.

Talia looked with the what the hell are you doing face. Knight asked for everyone's attention then he pulled out a piece of paper. This shit was crazy for him because it was only supposed to be him and Talia present when he proposed but he refused to hold it in any longer. She was his lady and fuck whoever had a problem with it.

"Can I get everyone's attention?" He repeated it a little louder this time. The crowd immediately faced him when they seen who it was. Talia smiled at the thought of how much a boss her man was. He had mad respect everywhere that he went.

"First off, I would like to thank you all for coming out tonight and supporting us but most of all I would like to thank my beautiful girl for making this all possible for a nigga. I mean for me, excuse my language." He gestured for Talia to come to him.

She had the most confused look on her face but she came to her man. He grabbed her hand and kissed it, she smiled. Knight opened up his paper then looked dead into her eyes then looked at the crowd and spoke.

"I wasn't expecting to be in front of all of ya'll either but I have a few words for my lady so...here it goes." He cleared his throat then began.

"Who knew....she'd make me think twice for the first time in a while make me think right. Thinking damn can this be right...fuck it I don't care i'm going out on a limb, emotions running so deep I could swim...cooler than an autumn breeze now i'm thinking that i'm falling. Don't know just yet but if I had to bet i'd be all in...who knew who knew in such a short time it'd be me and you...All I know is this is something I can do. Got me shaking my head, WHO KNEW!"

Once he was done Talia swelled up with tears of joy. She loved this man with all of her heart and here he was, on this stage in front of all of these people confessing his love for her. She held her hand over her mouth trying to regain her composure and then he pulled her close to him. He caught her off guard when he dropped down on one knee. Her heart was beating a mile a minute and so was his. In her head she was thinking this can't be true. In his head he was thinking that he couldn't believe that he was doing this. Knight could not find the right words so he sat there silent for a while with his head in her hands. He knew he wanted her to say yes but he never practiced what he would say to her.

Nikki was always extra and the silence was killing her. She just yelled "Oh my God! Propose to her already."

Knight smiled. It was now or never.

Black Angel

"Talia. I love you with all of my heart girl. I know I am not the easiest person to get along with but I am willing to work with you. We've been through so much and I can't see myself without you. I know you got my back and I got yours. And always remember...Love is NEVER painless baby but i'll never intentionally hurt you so bare with me. With all of that being said, will you marry me?"

With no hesitation she said, "Yes! Yes Knight, I will marry you."

She loved him but the last thing that she saw was herself forcing him to marry her. It was what she wanted but she needed it to come naturally and his timing was perfect. Things would not be all gravy but she was okay with that. As long as he was trying she was staying.

Knight pulled out the ring and all mouths dropped including his own. He forgot how gorgeous that bitch was his self. It was custom-made heart shaped diamond with two pear cuts on each side, 1.3 carat, with a platinum band. He spent some real cash on that ring and Talia was worth every thousand. Lalo was lightweight upset that Knight had been hiding this moment from him but he was happy for his friend. They would discuss that later. He held out his hand and she placed hers inside of it. Knight slid the ring on her finger and she dropped to her knees to kiss him. Their emotions were running wild. Half of the crowd was crying along with them. They got up and the DJ congratulated the couple then returned to the regular flow.

The crowd went crazy and they were all trying to get to the new Mr. and Mrs. Harris to tell them congratulations and to get a better look at that ring. Knight and Talia were rushed by groups of friends and family talking to them and they didn't even notice that a group of men was walking towards them. Knight heard the cocking of the gun and his first reaction was to yell "get down", push Talia to the ground, and pull out his own strap all in one motion. She had an instant flashback of the last encounter her and Knight had with guns. This time she wasn't faking and freezing up. She was definitely busting at whoever it was for fucking up their day.

As soon as he turned back around shots were being fired at him. Pow Pow! Knight let off his Glock 40, no safety and one of the niggas dropped. He noticed Lalo across the room bussing at them from a different direction. Lalo stayed ten toes down and solid. While Talia was on the ground she reached in her Chanel clutch and pulled out her 22 She then peeped the scene and hopped up to help her fiance. He was taking these niggas the fuck out. It had to be about 15 of them. The only thing that was going through Talia's head was how the fuck did they get past security. She didn't know but she would damn sure find out. What the fuck was she paying them for if they were protecting themselves anyway?

Knight was so into shooting the right people and keeping his family and friends safe that he hadn't noticed Talia standing right next to him shooting too. Then a familiar face caught her eye. It was Cordero. *What the hell is he doing here?* She hadn't seen him since her and Knight had been together. He left without explanation and she still wanted one but right now was not the time. *But why was he after Knight? Why here? Why today?* Her gun was pointed

Black Angel

right at Cordero when Knight had notied her. He thought that she had just froze up again so he took the shot but Cordero was already in motion. She couldn't bring herself to shoot him even though she really wanted to and probably needed to.

"Baby what are you doing?" He was yelling over all of the noise.

He had taken Talia the gun range numerous times with him and made her take self defense classes and he would do the same if he ever had a daughter. She needed to know how to defend herself in any situation and he needed to know that she would be able to take care of herself if he was not around.

"I needed to help you." She yelled back.

Knight was all for her helping as long as she understood the possible consequences but why did she freeze up was the question.

"Knight watch out!"

That was all Lalo got out before his friend hit the ground. One of the dudes caught him in the chest. Lalo came running from where he was shooting at with his gun out to rescue his best friend. Talia got down and put pressure on his wound. She was scared to death but was the most calm one there.

Lalo was acting a damn fool. He didn't know if he wanted to help Knight or kill who did this to him but he knew he had to act fast. She got his attention and had him to go call 911 then find Nikki and Kamari. Everything was happening so fast. The whole party was running wild. She kept her composure and stayed by her man's side.

"Help is coming baby. Just look at me. I am not going anywhere." She stayed by his side and assured him of that.

Nikki and Kamari came running over to her.

"Are you okay?" They asked in unison.

"I'm good. Here. Take these, go to my house, and put these in my safe."

She handed them her and Knight's gun and her keys. Nikki was the only one besides Knight and Talia who knew the combination to her safe. They ran out and headed straight to her house like she had requested. They knew that their friend could handle this so they were comfortable with leaving her there alone. She was far from a sucka and this was nothing to her. She just hoped that Knight would pull through this.

Knight started to lose consciousness and Talia could not do anything more but just keep him warm and talk to him until the ambulance arrived. The last thing that he remembered was hearing Talia talking to him. She kept repeating that she loved him and that everything would be alright then he blacked out. Soon after the ambulance arrived, asking a million and one questions. Knight wound up needing surgery and she stayed with him until he came out. Her clothes were filled with blood but she was not leaving him until she knew that he would have a full recovery. She dozed off after a while once she knew that Knight was okay and woke up with police in her face.

Black Angel

Chapter Fourteen

"Hello Ms. Smith." The police officer had a wide grin on his face. "It's Mrs. Harris now. How may I assist you?" She was very agitated.

"We're here to investigate the shooting that occurred last night during a party." The detective told her while writing notes in a notepad. Talia was no dummy and she knew that she did not have to tell them anything. All these snakes wanted to do was pin some bullshit on her and Knight to lock them up. They had been on his case for months but she would definitely play this cool.

"Well officer I am so sorry that you had to drive all the way down here for nothing but we don't have anything to tell you. All we know is some gang bangers ran up in our spot and shot at us." Talia used her sarcastic voice on them.

"So ma'am, you have no clue who these men were?"

"No sir." She played dumb.

"Well we have reason to believe that you two were some how connected to a drop off and shoot out that occurred about 7 months ago and we have a lead." He tried to set her up and get her to talk.

He thought that that she would break easy because Knight couldn't speak for her but she had it. She would never let them get any information out of her because real G's never fold.

"Shoot out and drop off? No sir I do not recall any of this that you are talking about."

"So what about Los and Red? Do those names mean anything to you?" He kept on trying.

Tay Sheree

She knew exactly what he was talking about and she couldn't wait until Knight woke up so she could let him know about this bullshit. How the fuck do they have us connected to this shit? She was thinking to herself.

"Officer as I told you before, I have no clue what you are talking about." Knight's phone began to ring.

"Now will you excuse me, I have to get this." She lied.

Talia reached on the stand and grabbed the phone. There was no name with the number but she answered anyways to get the police to stop talking to her.

"Hello. Talia speaking how may I help you?" She spoke into the phone.

It was silence for a moment then the voice on the other end finally said something.

"Where is Knight?" She had an attitude.

"And you are?" Talia spoke back.

"This is Ronnelle. Is Knight around? I need to speak to him. He still letting ya'll answer his phones. Ha!" She boldly spit at Talia knowing that Knight had just told her about Talia and tried to break it off between them.

She just wanted to start some shit. Knight pissed her off so somebody had to be mad with her.

"Look bitch! Knight is laid up in this bed and just got out of surgery so he'll have to call you later. And f.y.i i'm his fiancé sweetie so the next time you want to pop off i'll meet you where you stand." Talia hung up on the broad.

She was lightweight furious but she had to keep her cool with the police there. She turned her attention back to them.

Black Angel

"I am going to have to ask you to leave." She said calmly and walked away.

"If you come up with anything please call and let us know." Officer Williams told her as he held out a card for her. He needed to know everything that she knew before anyone else did. She gave him some evil eyes, he smiled and put the card on Knight's nightstand then him and his partner Davis left. Soon as they left she retrieved the number to this bitch who just made her mad. As soon as those pigs walked out Lalo walked in.

"I said I would call if I come up with anything!" Talia was yelling thinking that the cops had come back.

"Damn Li. Chill. It's only me."

"My bad. These fuckin' cops just left. They were questioning me and shit about the shooting."

"You didn't tell them anything did you?" Lalo had to be sure.

"Come on now! You know me better than that." She was pissed at the fact that he would even come at her side ways like that.

He was still mad as fuck about Knight being shot so he had to question everybody and see what the streets were talking about immediately. As he sat next to Knight's bed he ordered security to come be at Knight's door for protective purposes or just in case he needed to leave his side. He needed to be guarded at all times after this. Lalo doubted if them dumb fucks tried some shit like that anyways but it's always better to be safe than sorry. Talia sat across from him and called up her girls to bring her some clothes. She felt so filthy because she was still covered in blood from the shootout.

After a few days of recovery with Talia and Lalo being back and forth to the hospital the nurse finally came in with some good news. She informed them that Knight was officially out of the woods and stable enough to go home. The doctor came in one final time to tell him that he would make a full recovery with little to no complications and no further surgery should be needed. She gave him the aftercare instructions and had Knight sign his release papers He was blessed because the bullet that almost took him out was very close to his heart.

"Whelp. Look at that. You get to go home." She was happy but more tired of being cooped up in that little ass room.

"Yea. We both get to go home and get some rest. But you know I won't get no real rest until I handle whoever is responsible for this shit. I missed out on a couple dollars." One thing he hated was to lose money.

"Right. But you know we gone get that right back but I need to go check on the house and make sure the girls handled some business for me." She made up a lie.

She had already known that they had done what she had asked because they had been texting nonstop since Knight was admitted.

"That's cool. Lalo here. Gone head baby just hit me up later." She left and headed home but not for what she told him. She was still in rage but she hid that shit from him well. Before she spoke to him about it she had to do some research of her own.

Black Angel

When she left Knight was left there to do a little thinking of his own and to talk to his best friend about the past few days. He was mad as hell that he had to be laid up in the hospital on his birthday. When he got out he would get answers. Who the fuck was bold enough to run up in his party and shoot him? His phone kept beeping as a reminder letting him know that he had an unread text message. The sound was annoying him so he checked it even though he didn't really care about it. The message was from Ronnelle.

So now you are letting Talia answer yo phone. She must really be special to you. Don't think i'm letting go that easy! The bitch was clearly crazy. Knight's blood was boiling and he was confused as to when the hell Talia had answered his phone then not say anything to him about it. Now he was wondering why Talia hadn't said anything to him about it. This was just one fucked up day for him. But he put his phone back down because he wasn't in the mood to explain shit to anybody.

As she rode home she thought about what the officers had said. She remembered the lick that they had hit very clearly but what the fuck did these snakes know and how did they get any information? Just then she remembered the vice car that pulled up as they were leaving out. They were on the scene real quick. As bad as she wanted to talk to Knight about everything that she was thinking she was furious with him right now and until she had proof of something then she wasn't speaking on it. The next person on her list that she wanted to run to was Navy and the last time she had checked they were lightweight beefing. She starting blowing his phone up but was not getting an answer. She just noticed that her best friend had not called her and that was suspect. She knew no matter how mad they were they would always keep in touch. She called his son's mother and found out that he hadn't called her to pick up Martin either. So she went to the next option and just went by his house. Before she hopped out she grabbed her spare 9mm that she kept under her seat in her vehicle.

When she arrived she banged as hard as she could, gun still drawn, but got no answer then she went to the back door and shot the lock off. Her spare key to his house was on the chain that she gave Nikki and Kamari. She never thought she would ever have to do this and she hated that she did. She used her spare that Navy gave her and opened the door. When she entered the house she did it with much caution and she took a deep breath. She never put her gun down. Everything was still intact so you clearly knew that he wasn't robbed. Talia walked in and out of every room in the house and then his bedroom. She couldn't believe what she was doing. She slowly pushed the door open and seen that no one was there and she was relieved. Before she sat down she checked the closet and under the bed and it was all normal. Talia plopped right on Navy's king sized bed.

Where are you?" She whispered as a tear rolled down her face.

Talia hoped that she had not run him away because she needed him most right now. So much was going on and she needed to let it out.

Black Angel

She laid back and then she saw a notebook on his nightstand. She picked it up and began glancing through it. Not only was her best friend a photographer, he could write poems, and draw. He was the ultimate artist. She admired him for everything that he does and now she wished that she had went to L.A. with him instead of staying here for the bullshit. Every page of this book was filled with drawings and what looked like poems and she figured they were his thoughts so she kept going. Then one of the pages caught her eye. It was the very final page written on and it was addressed to her and dated for the day that he had left. She sat and read the whole thing. When she was done she was heated but at the same time in tears. She couldn't believe what she had just read and she needed answers asap. As she sat up and tried to breathe she had to think about what her next move would be. Whatever it may be she had to play it cool.

Chapter Fifteen

In L.A. The police were called to the scene of a warehouse. The owner was on his way in to do paper work when he spotted someone tied to a chair. He went running to help but it was beyond too late. The male had slits on both of his heels and he was stripped. He was beat so bad that you could barely identify him. Whoever did this was sick as hell. They were bold enough to take gruesome pictures of the torturing and laid them all around the warehouse where Navy was. They topped it off by leaving his camera around his neck. His clothes were found in dumpster a few blocks away and the police were able to identify him.

The LAPD contacted Cleveland police and let them know that they would be conducting an autopsy then they would release his body. The first place that Cleveland went was to his house to see if he had any relatives. They knocked several times and Talia was shook. She had her gun drawn, luckily it was her registered one, and she went to the door and opened it. When the police saw that she was armed they drew their guns on her and she put hers down instantly.

"Ma'am what is going on here?" They asked as they stepped inside of the house.

"Are you alone?"

"Yes, I am here alone. I came here to look for my best friend and I can't find him. Do you know where he is?" She was crying hysterically again.

Tay Sheree

"Does Navy Scott have any relatives that live here?" They were looking around the house for any signs of a second party.

"No. They're all out of town. I am the closest thing that he has to family. What the fuck is going on?" She was now screaming.

There was so much confusion in her voice.

"Ma'am, calm down. What is your name?"

"Talia. Talia Harris" she told him. She still wasn't sure if she should use Knight's last name. She wasn't sure of anything right now.

"We are not supposed to do this seeing that you are not his immediate family but someone has to be notified." He took a deep breath then found the guts to tell her.

"Can you sit down?" He tried to calm her nerves.

"Fuck sitting down. What do you have to tell me? Notify me of what? Is he in jail? What's his bail? Whatever the fuck it is I got it. Tell me!" She demanded.

"Talia, Navy was found dead in California." Talia passed out.

There was nothing more for them to say. Her world was crushed. This had been the worst 24 hours of her life. Her brain could not register all of this that was happening to her.

This couldn't be true. Talia was awakened by the officers and placed on Navy's couch before they continued to talk to her. They gave her details and she was distraught and now crying hysterically. *Who in the hell would kill Navy and why? He didn't do anything to anyone. He went out there for a showcase.*

Black Angel

"I can't deal with this." She got up and left.

She went straight to her new home and jumped in the shower. All she could do was cry. She washed her hair and pulled all of it up in a bun. She threw on a Guess jogging suit and she headed out to find some shit out. This shit was getting out of hand. Everything around her seemed to get worse by the minute. As she searched for the keys to her Impala she called Knight's phone. She called at least ten times with no answer.

"Why is this happening to me?" She threw her phone and sat on the couch.

"I was just proposed to, my fiancé was shot and now Navy is dead." She talked out loud to herself because she felt like she had lost it.

It had to be a dream. She could not do anything but believe it was all her fault. If she would not have planned this party Navy would not have been alone and Knight would not have been shot.

She fell asleep after sitting there thinking and when she woke up she rolled over and grabbed her phone. She looked over her missed calls and texts. Knight had called her several times then he text her. She freshened up then rushed home in hopes of him being there waiting for her. As she was walking to her vehicle her phone rang.

"Hello." She answered.

"This is global tel-link. You have a prepaid call from... Knight." The automated voice said to her.

She couldn't believe it. Knight was really in jail. She accepted his call then waited for him to speak.

"Hello, Talia. Where are you?"

"I'm leaving the hospital. I was looking for you. What happened?"

"I woke up in the hospital and two police officers were standing over me saying that they were there to arrest me. I'm down here on some fucking drug trafficking, robbery, and a possible murder charge. They're saying that they have a witness that placed me at the scene of some drop where some people were killed" He told her this knowing that she would know exactly what he was talking about.

"You need to keep me updated. I have a lot that I have to handle out here. They found Navy dead in L.A.!" She bust out in tears all over again.

She couldn't believe that she was even saying this.

"Damn baby. That's fucked up. You cool?" He tried to sound as sympathetic as possible even knowing the foul shit that he had done. It took everything in him to do this but he had to. He couldn't have Navy messing up what him and Talia had built.

After he caught Navy sneaking up on him in Cali he had to send one of his soldiers out to get him. It didn't even have to end like that though.

"I'm through out here. I can't take this Knight. I need you but I have to stay strong right now for the both of us."

Talia held weight for her and Knight and he respected her for it. She was way stronger both mentally and physically than any other female that he had ever come across.

Black Angel

"Shit fucked up right now but we gone get through this. I have to call Lalo so go home and get some rest. We gone handle this."

"I love you Knight."

"I love you too Talia."

Rest was the last thing on her mind. She tried to hate Knight now but she was a firm believer of believing half of what you hear and all of what you see.

Even still she had to remain solid through it all and hold her man down regardless of the circumstances.

Going through her contact list she came across the number of exactly who she needed to be in contact with. Knight gave Talia Shauntille's number so she could represent him when he got in some bullshit and couldn't speak for himself. Shauntille is the paralegal at Knight's lawyer's office that she had to call and inform that Knight had been arrested.

"Hi. Shauntille. This is Knight's fiancé. I was calling because"...

"Say no more. I am going to make a few calls, do up this paperwork for the lawyer and we will have him back to you in the morning. Go and meet him downtown"

Shauntille had only cut Talia off because everything that she was going to tell her she would find out and they would be wasting time. Knight didn't give a fuck about charges just as long as he wasn't sitting in a cell. He had the best lawyer out there and he made sure that they were paid well. Talia still felt like they were fucking because Shauntille is always very quick when it comes to Knight. He either fucking her good to pay her off and get the job done or the bitch is just really about her business. That was irrelevant right now though. Talia needed Knight back out on the streets with her.

Chapter Sixteen

Today was the day of Navy's funeral at The Word Church. Talia tried to keep her composure but it was killing her. The service was very nice and she had Nikki and Kamari right by her side to comfort her. Shauntille kept her word and Knight was out that next morning. He was at the funeral too holding Talia up as she balled just from the sight of the casket, showing no remorse. Talia couldn't bear the fact that it was a closed casket. The day before, she had to pay the funeral director to let her see Navy before the funeral. Whoever did this would suffer just as much as Navy did if not worse. How could someone be so cruel and kill Navy? They fucked up her world. The whole time that she was sitting there she was plotting. When all of this blew over she was going into investigative bitch mode. Speaking of bitch, she still had something for the hoe that got tough with her over Knight's phone. Anybody could catch it right about now.

After the funeral the repast was to be held in the skate hall at the church. Talia didn't stay long because she wanted to go home and mourn the loss of her best friend alone. She had huge canvasses of his work set up all over. She knew that his passion was photography so she honored him by decorating her basement for him. She had huge pictures of her and Knight put up too. She needed good memories in her thoughts right now. Her favorite was the picture of Navy and Martin. They looked so happy, now he has to grow up without his father. She would never forget her best friend.

Tay Sheree

As she admired all of the canvasses she heard footsteps coming down the basement stairs. She wasn't expecting anyone to be there. She cocked her gun and aimed right for the stair case.

"Relax. Who else would be in our house?" Knight walked toward her and sat on the couch.

"By the way you did a nice job picking this house out by yourself. I like it." He told her.

"Thank you." Talia had only told Lalo about the house because they were only giving him a spare key. When Knight was released from the hospital Lalo had took Knight there since Talia wasn't answering her phone.

He just sat there and watched her. He knew that she would speak when she was ready.

"What are you doing here so early? I thought you and Lalo were taking care of some business."

Knight and Lalo had gone to the hood after the funeral to see what the streets would give them about the shooting. It did not even take long because somebody was always running their mouth.

"Yea. That's what I came here to talk to you about. I found out everything that I needed to know. Now I just have to confirm it." He hoped that she would get the hint and start talking but she just gave a look as if to say, *what the fuck are you talking about*.

"That's what's up. I want these niggas dead."

"That's a done deal. My part is done. Now it's time for you to do yours." He had her full attention now. She was confused.

Black Angel

"Alright. Cut the bullshit. What is really on your mind? You startin' to blow the fuck out of me."

"Right. Right. So, who the fuck is Cordero and why the fuck is that nigga shooting at us? Better yet, why didn't you kill the bitch nigga when your gun was aimed at him?" Knight stood up, still mad about the whole situation.

"An old friend." She never made eye contact with him and she knew that he hated that shit.

Grabbing her face he turned her around to look him dead in his face. "Talia look at me when i'm fuckin' talkin' to you."

She took off on him and punched him dead in his face. She had so much animosity built up that it was just a reflex. His natural reflex was to smack the shit out of her. She flew back and landed on her back. She went to jump up and swing on him again but he was already on the floor pinning her down.

"Baby I am sorry!" He kissed her face as tears swelled up in her eyes. "We need to talk, this is serious."

She wouldn't dare lie to his face. How do you respect someone after that?

"Okay. I used to fuck with him back in the day. Nothing serious but he's really just an old friend. I promise."

"Fuck you mean an old friend Talia? That nigga ran up in our party a shot at us but you gon' look me in my face and tell me that he a friend." He let her arms go and shook his head at her. "Old friend or not that nigga tried to kill us. Yo stupid ass was obviously too caught up in your feelings to notice that!" He was yelling at her as she stood there showing no emotion. She was so numb that nothing phased her.

"Dead that nigga Talia! You really don't want me to get involved." He walked back upstairs to roll his blunt as he left her where she was standing to let what he said to her marinate.

Talia knew exactly what she had to do. She called up Kamari and Nikki to give the scoop on what needed to be done. Her bitches were always down to ride, well Kamari anyway. Nikki was good at keeping secrets but she wasn't the one for catching a body.

Later that night her and her girls stepped out to Kings and Queens. It was a Friday night so it was not that crowded and that was perfect for the occasion. They sat at the bar and Talia said fuck ordering drink by drink. She needed to be in control of her own liquor so she ordered two bottles for her and her girls. They sat and drank for hours until Talia was numb. She was already high from the Kush blunt that she smoked on her way there so she was for sure feeling herself. She felt like she had got drunk faster than usual today so she quit and headed to the dance floor.

"Come on ya'll. We gotta fuck it up for my best friend" She was on one.

Navy would usually be by her side acting a fool and in her mind he was. Even though she was in pain too she did not let that show. She needed to have some type of fun or at least fake like she was. Music always took her away from her problem plus she had to get ready for the plan that her and her girls had set up for when they left the bar.

Black Angel

After a long night of drinking and dancing they headed to Kamari's house. They all got undressed and laid around until Talia gave Kamari the heads up that it was time for what they had discussed. After about an hour or so, Talia decided that she was ready. There was no sense in prolonging the situation, it had to happen. First she had to run to the bathroom to go pee. Her bladder was full as hell from drinking all of that liquor and Red Bulls. On the way to the bathroom she whispered to Kamari.

"When Nikki falls asleep it's on."

Kamari gave her the head nod.

Looking at her phone she began to dial a number. When she got drunk she always called up Knight and whined to him about nothing but this time it was all on her. She thought about the conversation that they had earlier and continued to dial the number. He was already mad at her too so that was out of the question. Talia would stay where she was until his request was fulfilled. She found herself calling Navy. She broke down and cried because he always knew what to say when she needed help or just someone to be there. *Fuck that i'm calling. Suck this shit up Talia. You know what you have to do. Why would that motherfucka' think he would get away with this shit anyways.* It ain't nothing like a little liquid encouragement. Talia poured herself a shot of Henn and redialed the correct number this time.

Putting the phone on speaker oddly made her feel better so she sat the phone down and listened to it ring. She watched the phone as it rang once, then twice, and on the third ring a male picked up the phone. Out of nowhere she got real confident. It was Cordero.

"Hello. What's up. Can you meet up with me?" Talia spoke and waited for a reply.

Cordero knew that he had owed her an explanation as to why he bailed out on her but he always kept in mind that he did shoot at her.

"Yea. I can. What's up?"

"I think we both know what's up. You know that we have some things to discuss." She played it off real smooth.

She hung up the phone without even stating her location knowing that he already knew. He accepted her offer so easily because of their history together. Ever since they had first started talking Cordero made sure he knew Talia's whereabouts because it was a few people at her neck. He put her on to the game so he would always have her back as he had promised her. Talia would never let Knight know this because Cordero never made his presence known. He just pulled up on scenes to make sure that she was good. Sometimes he would go unnoticed and others she would peep him.

Cordero was so anxious to meet up with Talia and she was ready to get it over with. He knew that she was a down ass bitch and apparently this dope boy named Knight had her mind for the moment. Cordero felt that Talia was his first, so if he wanted her back then that would be no problem. He was a selfish dude and he wanted whatever Talia and Knight had to end. He figured since she had not shot him at the party that she still had feelings for him. But most importantly he needed to meet up with her

Black Angel

to find out where the fuck his money was. He turned his radio up, lit his blunt and headed to Kamari's house.

Talia threw on some clothes and headed downstairs as she waited for Cordero to arrive. His headlights grew bright then quickly went away as he pulled into the driveway. She watched him as he got out of the car and the feeling that came over her was awkward. The sight of him was making her moist. She couldn't tell if the alcohol had her feeling like this or just him.

He was half Spanish and half black. His skin had a reddish color to it that glistened when the sun hit him. He was slim only weighing 200 lbs. His face hair and chin hair was tapered, he always kept it clean. Women always complimented him on his hair so he kept his naturally curly hair trimmed low at the top. His laid back swag was what always turned her on to him. A hood man with a nice ass body was her weakness.

When she opened the door he stood there all of 6 feet even in his gray polo jogging pants. His white v neck cut low enough to show his tattoo on his collar bone that said *Loyalty over all*. That was her favorite tattoo on him out his 76 that he had all over his body. On his feet he wore some wheat Timberlands that look so perfect on his size 11's. She loved his style.

"What do you want to talk about?" He got straight to the point.

She chuckled as she stepped out of the door and lightly closed it. She had to give the appearance that she did not want to wake her friends. They were wide awoke, ready for action. She stepped in front of him and led him to the back patio. As they walked to the back he watched her ass move in her pajama shorts as he listened to her tell him her whole situation with her and Knight. Talia expressed all of her feelings that came with Navy's death and how crazy her life has been ever since. Her mind was so fucked up at this point that she spilled her heart out to the man that she was sent to kill by her fiancé.

He listened to every word that she had to say and gave her a decent amount of feedback. She knew Cordero like the back of her hand just as well as he knew her. The fact that he was trying to act all tough toward her cracked her up. Playing along with him was just a part of her sick twisted pleasure.

"So, who do you think has something to do with Navy's death? That shit don't sound like no accident."

"Who the fuck you telling? Just believe me when I tell you that as soon as I find out who ever did this will pay!"

She felt herself getting caught up in her feelings so she quickly switched the subject.

"Why were you at the party?" She had to get back to business.

"Man. Truthfully yo nigga Knight ain't who you think he is. He stole some money and merchandise from me and I need that shit back." Talia wanted to shoot him right then and there for coming at her like that but that would be too easy.

"Oh really! What he owe you?" She sat there and listened to his lies for the last time and got even more mad by the second. He was full of shit and her loyalty was with

Black Angel

Knight no matter what Cordero said so this motherfucker had to go.

After sitting down on the porch swing Cordero got real comfortable and laid across her lap. Her first mind told her to push him off but she just relaxed and let him lay there. She closed her eyes and thought about all of the times that they used to get high and just chill but this would be the last time that Cordero would get to chill with anyone.

"Roll up." She needed to ease her mind. He sat up and did what he was told.

He smoked so much that he already had another blunt rolled. He lit it then passed it to Talia. She sat on the edge of the swing and hit the blunt four times. They smoked the whole blunt then sat there stuck for a minute. That Kush always put them on their ass and she loved the feeling. Talia knew that sooner than later he would get horny and he was right on que. When she looked over Cordero sat dick in hand slowly massaging it. She took a deep breath and did what she had to. *Alright Talia. Let's do this.*

She stood up and stepped right in front on him and stood in between his legs. Leaning over, she planted a kiss right on his soft lips and his jacked his dick faster then harder. He pulled her to his face then kissed her back. He rubbed his hands all over her body then smacked her ass so hard that she screamed a little. He hadn't seen her in a while and she was turning him on to the max. He instructed her to take off her clothes and she did as she was told. He grabbed her hand and walked her naked body over to the stairs. He pulled his jogging pants and boxers down then parted her legs. He parted her ass cheeks then smacked them one by one. He still remembered that she liked to be fucked rough.

He pushed her back down and guided his piece to her vagina. He rubbed the head of it in circles on her clit and she squealed. He wanted to tease her a little bit before he gave her what she really wanted. She used to use the rest of the niggas out here but Cordero was always there to fuck her, smoke with her, and assist her with business. Now it was time to get down to business. He touched her pussy to make sure that it was ready for him then rammed his dick inside of her causing her to damn near fall. She let out a scream that she could not hold in even if she wanted to.

The patio door slid open making no sound and a person walked out. Cordero heard a board from the porch squeak but that never stopped his flow. Kamari walked out never saying a word but she sat in a chair and watched for a moment. Watching how Cordero was pounding her friend, making her ass shake was sexy as hell to her. She stepped on the side of Cordero whispered something in his ear then handed him a glass. He slowed his pace, took a sip of his drink, and then followed her order. She tipped her glass back and took a sip of her wine too. Cordero went to sit down and Kamari went to take a stand behind Talia to get a better view of what Cordero was getting a piece of. Talia looked back at her because this wasn't a part of their plan but she didn't want to be so obvious and ask what she was doing so she played along.

Black Angel

Kamari decided to switch it up a little, never altering their original scheme. She squatted down then using only her tongue she sucked Talia's pussy from the back. They were both letting out moans like crazy and Cordero sat and watched with his drink in one hand and dick in the other. He never knew that Talia was into this type of shit. He could lightweight tell that she wasn't but at this point she couldn't deny the feeling. Kamari had her making noises that even he hadn't heard from her before. After Kamari felt Talia's knees buckle she stood up to give her a break as she planted soft kisses all down her back. Talia wasn't gay or anything but her best friend had her feeling so good that she didn't want her to stop. Then Kamari grabbed Talia by her thigh and placed her leg in a hair leaving her legs spread apart. She slid one, then two fingers inside of her and worked them as she used her free hand to play with her clit and she started hollering all over again. Kamari whispered in her ear as she pleased her heightening the moment.

"You gone cum for me Talia?"

She found her spot and hit it with her two fingers until that bitch came all over her hand. Her legs were trembling so much afterward that she hit the deck and they both laughed. She extended her hand and helped Talia up and she gave her the "bitch let's get back to business look." They got it together and walked over to Cordero. He was still sitting there sipping his drink just enjoying their little show.

"Drink up." Kamari said as she stood and watched him.

Tay Sheree

He swallowed the last of his concoction and they both sat back and waited for the effects of it.

"You feeling it yet?" Talia asked.

He was now feeling the effect of the Doxacurium. Kamari spiked his wine before she came out. Cordero was seeing double, then triple.

"What the fuck ya'll bitches do to me?" His body was shutting down.

"Well Cordero, you see what you drank was a mixture of wine and a neuromuscular blocker and what you are experiencing is paralysis." By now he was no longer able to speak.

Cordero was losing his ability to breathe. Talia and Kamari were watching him silently plead for his life.

Out of nowhere the sliding doors opened once again, this time with Nikki appearing. Talia and Kamari looked at each other shocked. Talia tried to stand in front of Cordero to block Nikki's view.

"What's taking so long?" Nikki finally spoke.

Again with confused looks on their faces they all turned around to check on Cordero.

Tears slowly rolled down his face as his eyes began to roll to the back of his head.

"I see that you are all in your feelings so let me help you with this." Talia felt feelings that she knew she needed to get rid of and there was no turning back from what she had already started. Nikki looked her friend in the eyes as to show her where her loyalty lies.

Nikki wasn't as conservative as they had thought that she was.

Black Angel

She walked around him in the chair and stood behind him. She grabbed his chin and pulled his head back as far as she could. Reaching under her pant leg she pulled out her Butterfly knife that never left her side and slit Cordero's throat from ear to ear. She kept his head back so that it would be quick and easy. His blood squirted all over the patio. Talia threw up while Nikki ran in the house to jump in the shower. Kamari was already starting to clean up the mess. None of them could believe that what they had just did but it had to be done.

"Alright. I'm good." Talia walked back over toward his limp body and got sick again.

"Let's go!" Kamari had to prompt her to finish what they had started.

They had to dispose of his body and clean up all of the evidence thoroughly and Talia drove his car to do it. Nikki followed them with her car to drive them all back home. Kamari drove Talia's truck because she had not got rid of it yet. Cordero fucked with the wrong ones. Loyalty is everything!

Chapter Seventeen

After a long night of disposing Cordero's body Talia headed home to her fiancé. She knew that without Knight saying many words that he wanted Cordero dead and she had to make that happen. That morning Talia was woke out of her sleep by a sharp pain in her side. These pains kept coming back and she had enough of that shit. When she rolled over to get out of bed Knight felt her and immediately jumped up to question her.

"What's up?"

"Shit." She knew exactly what he wanted to hear but she decided to be stubborn.

"That's how you feel?" He was tired of her playing crazy.

"It's done. It's over with. You have nothing else to worry about."

He didn't care about anything else that she had to say nor was he worried. He would handle the rest of Cordero's people sooner than later. He heard what he needed to from Talia. The moment that she would have told him that she did not take care of it Knight was going to handle the both of them. He needed to know where the loyalty of his bitch was. He knew that she had feelings for that nigga Cordero but it was either him or Knight. He refused to be an option. He was going to take the nigga out regardless though for shooting at him but he rather Talia do it to test her.

Tay Sheree

She brushed her teeth, and then showered. She sped over to their other house to grab a few things. On her way there she called to make an appointment with her doctor because she was tired of this pain and had been ignoring it for too long. When she got up to her house and put the key in the door she noticed a large manila envelope in the mailbox. She ignored it and continued to go in the house because she was still on the phone with the receptionist.

"Yes! I need to come in as soon as possible. What do you mean my doctor is booked until next week? There are a million fucking people in there. Choose one and schedule me!" She was heated and in pain at the same time so she was taking it out on the lady over the phone.

She grabbed what she needed then headed right back out the door. After locking up she picked up all of the mail that had accumulated since they had been gone. She thumbed through a bunch of bills and irrelevant stuff then she made it to the manila envelope that was addressed to her. Her stomach dropped to her feet when she read the sender name. The letter was from Navy Scott.

"What the fuck is going on?" She looked around her yard and up the street hoping that someone was playing a sick ass joke on her.

She began to cry as she opened up the package that was supposedly from her deceased best friend. Her mind raced as she braced herself for what she was about to see. *Why the fuck did he send me mail from out there. He should have brought it home to me. What was so important?* She was confused as to how he sent a return address because he did not know anyone who lived out there. At the same time she

Black Angel

was heated because she knew that if he had to send mail that he knew he would not be coming back.

Talia never went directly to thinking positively about a situation because a what if question always came to her head. Then when she reached her hand in the envelope she found herself pulling out a small stack of pictures. She wanted to believe that they would be shots of his work from the showcase but she hoped for the best and prepared for the worst.

The first picture in the stack was a picture of Knight walking up to a house.

"What is this about?" She sucked up tears as her heart started beating faster and faster.

The second one was of him and a beautiful woman walking out of the same house. Then the third was of Knight, the woman, and a little boy. As she stared at it, it seemed as if Knight was looking dead at the camera. She was done. She opened up her door and threw up all in her drive way. The way that she was feeling she could have drove back home and killed Knight herself. It all made sense now. Navy had been trying to give her clues the whole time but she was not listening. She let her love for Knight blind her. He caught her slipping but she had something for him. She had to confront him immediately.

She threw the envelope on the seat and all the mail fell on the floor. When she finished picking them up she saw a letter that said *Department of Child and Family Services of L.A.* They had to have the wrong house. Then she looked again and the name said Knight Harris.

Tay Sheree

"You have got to be fucking kidding me." She furiously opened the letter and tried to read it carefully.

She was so mad that she could not even focus. Fuck everything else that the letter was talking about. All she saw was 99.999% the biological father of Sharod Harris and she lost it. This had to be a joke. He had a kid on her and failed to mention it, or did he even know about this was the better question.

Many thoughts went through her mind. All of this time Knight knew that she wanted a family and even promised her one when they were *ready*. How could he betray her? He was always giving her some bullshit excuse as to why they should wait and maybe that was because he knew that he already had a child to take care of. She was livid. This bitch nigga was out here living a double life while she was at home playing house giving this nigga her all. But she gave it to him. He played the shit off pretty damn well but the pictures and the DNA test did it for her. No longer was she in pain, she was in rage. Everyone who ever crossed her would pay! Talia was coming for blood, fuck explanations. It has been too late for all that shit.

Her heart turned cold. No longer did she care about anything or anyone. She didn't care what she had to do or who she had to kill to get answers. Talia was back and with a vengeance. These past weeks had her out of her hook up and it was time for her to take control again. She was proposed to by a cheater who has been living a double life, her best friend was murdered, Knight was looking at jail time, and she had become a murderer.

Black Angel
She called Nikki and Kamari on three way. She wasted no time when they answered their phone.
"Aye! I'm thinking vacation. Ya'll down?"
"Hell yea! Where to?" You could hear her friends excitement through the phone.
"Cali, baby." Talia told her friends.
She wasn't quite ready to let them know details yet but they would know soon. She did not need them over reacting for her.

First she gets pictures in the mail of Knight, a bitch, and some kid mailed to her by Navy. Then coincidently Navy gets murdered in L.A. when he goes out for his show. *Somebody tryna play me for a fuckin' fool and something is definitely going on.* She headed home to order their tickets and plot some more. The first place that she planned ongoing when they touched down was Los Angeles police department to find out any further details to Navy's case. She sat the pictures in front of her on the computer desk to get another look at them as she waited for the plane tickets to process. She noticed something that would take her exactly where she needed to be. Navy was one smart man. She dried her face and put on a devilish grin. Navy was hipped to Talia's lifestyle so he had to put clues in ways that only she would understand. This clue cleared up all of her confusion.

Navy clearly caught Knight in his act. *When Knight caught Navy it wasn't because he was trying to get a close up of him, he was getting a good shot of the address that Knight was at.* She looked at the envelope again and sure enough the return address was right where Knight stood. She had

Tay Shereé

every intention of going directly to that house. She would find out everything that she needed to know.

Fuck Love! What is that? I gave him my ALL. I was once a good girl but now it's no turning back. I'll show him the true meaning of a Black Angel.

CHANGE THE GAME
THE SEQUEL TO
Black Angel
BY
Tay Shereé
COMING SOON

About the author

Tay Shereé born and raised in Cleveland, Ohio, is a mother of one beautiful son, Rashad Sincere O'Neal. Writing has been a passion of hers since grade school and now she has finally decided to share her talents with the world.

Feel free to follow this rising Author @
Mz.bgsu@gmail.com
IG black_an9el
facebook Taylor Shereé
Twitter Str8_LikeDat_

Made in the USA
Columbia, SC
22 April 2018